The Dead Heat of Summer

Also from Heather Graham

Slow Burn
Night Heat

The Dead Heat of Summer

A Krewe of Hunters Novella

By Heather Graham

1001 DARK NIGHTS
PRESS

The Dead Heat of Summer
A Krewe of Hunters Novella
Copyright 2020 Heather Graham Pozzessere

ISBN: 978-1-951812-19-5

Foreword: Copyright 2014 M. J. Rose

Published by 1001 Dark Nights Press, an imprint of Evil Eye Concepts, Incorporated

Sign up for the 1001 Dark Nights Newsletter
and be entered to win a Tiffany Key necklace.

There's a contest every month!

Go to www.1001DarkNights.com to subscribe!

**As a bonus, all subscribers can download
FIVE FREE exclusive books!**

One Thousand and One Dark Nights

Once upon a time, in the future…

*I was a student fascinated with stories and learning.
I studied philosophy, poetry, history, the occult, and
the art and science of love and magic. I had a vast
library at my father's home and collected thousands
of volumes of fantastic tales.*

*I learned all about ancient races and bygone
times. About myths and legends and dreams of all
people through the millennium. And the more I read
the stronger my imagination grew until I discovered
that I was able to travel into the stories… to actually
become part of them.*

*I wish I could say that I listened to my teacher
and respected my gift, as I ought to have. If I had, I
would not be telling you this tale now.
But I was foolhardy and confused, showing off
with bravery.*

*One afternoon, curious about the myth of the
Arabian Nights, I traveled back to ancient Persia to
see for myself if it was true that every day Shahryar
(Persian: شهريار, "king") married a new virgin, and then
sent yesterday's wife to be beheaded. It was written
and I had read that by the time he met Scheherazade,
the vizier's daughter, he'd killed one thousand
women.*

*Something went wrong with my efforts. I arrived
in the midst of the story and somehow exchanged
places with Scheherazade — a phenomena that had
never occurred before and that still to this day, I
cannot explain.*

*Now I am trapped in that ancient past. I have
taken on Scheherazade's life and the only way I can
protect myself and stay alive is to do what she did to
protect herself and stay alive.*

*Every night the King calls for me and listens as I spin tales.
And when the evening ends and dawn breaks, I stop at a
point that leaves him breathless and yearning for more.
And so the King spares my life for one more day, so that
he might hear the rest of my dark tale.*

*As soon as I finish a story... I begin a new
one... like the one that you, dear reader, have before
you now.*

Prologue

July

She was beautiful in death, as she had always been in life.

Lena Marceau lay with her blond hair fanned out like silk on the pillow. She wore a white nightgown.

Her hands were folded just below her breasts. She could have been an angel sleeping, filled with light and peace.

Ryder McKinley looked down at her, feeling numb.

"The medical examiner is ready to take the body," Braxton Wild told him.

Braxton was a detective with the New Orleans Police Department and had called Ryder. He was also one of the few people who knew there was an association between Ryder and Lena Marceau.

He had reached out to Ryder after Stephanie Harrow called him. She had been the one to find her sister. Had told Braxton that she'd gone to the house and assumed that since the baby was napping, her sister was, too. But after about thirty minutes, she realized that Lena wasn't just sleeping.

She was dead.

Stephanie was, of course, a mess. She was ready to take care of Lena's two-year-old daughter, Annette, but she had been crying so hard, she'd had to call in a friend—Vickie Carmichael—to take the child.

Before Ryder even reached the Marceau mansion, Stephanie had been sedated, and she and the baby had been whisked off to Vickie's house in the French Quarter.

There was no sign of any kind of trauma on the body; no sign of a break-in. Ryder knew Dr. Hugh Lamont, the medical examiner, and Braxton believed that Lena had committed suicide. Bottles of prescription medicine lay at her side. One was a strong sleeping pill she had started taking when her husband died a year ago.

Through her husband, Lena was the heir to a great estate. Not that there weren't other members of the Marceau family, but old Elijah Marceau had died just before his great-grandson, and he had loved Anthony and Lena.

They had loved him, too. Not only his money.

Lena had never been one to care about material things.

Ryder and Lena hadn't been able to catch up in a few years. When he'd been in NOLA recently, she had been in Europe. But they had communicated now and then on the phone, though mostly through email or social media.

"Ryder?"

"Yes, of course," he said, moving aside.

The memory of her, so angelic, would live in his mind forever.

He kept his face impassive as he asked, "The autopsy will be in the morning?"

"Yes."

"You won't mind if I attend?" Ryder asked Braxton.

"No, of course not," Braxton said and then hesitated. "We've worked with your Krewe people from the get-go down here, so my lieutenant had no problem with me inviting you along on a…routine investigation."

"Thanks."

"Ryder, it looks like suicide," Braxton said sadly. "Maybe she just couldn't endure the loss of her husband."

Ryder gave him a rueful smile. "No. Lena loved Anthony very much, and she mourned him deeply. But she was a mother, Braxton."

"Mothers aren't immune to the depression that kills," Braxton said gently.

"I don't believe it," Ryder asserted.

"Ryder, if all the M.E. finds is a mixture of her prescription drugs in her system, we're going to have no choice but to call it a suicide."

"Yes, I know."

"Oh. Okay," Braxton said.

Ryder gave him his best smile. "I'll be there tomorrow. I know what we're all expecting, but I'll be there."

"When do you go back to headquarters?"

"I have some time. We just chased down that drug runner who was targeting teens in the Southern cities. I have a bit of leave. I'll be around."

"I was afraid of that."

Ryder smiled.

"I won't step on local police. I'll be an angel," he said.

Then Ryder thought of her again. His beautiful, young cousin, lying there as if her dreams were sweet and wonderful.

Yes, an angel.

She had mourned her husband. Lena had loved Anthony. And he had loved her because what they shared hadn't been about the Marceau name or the money.

She had his daughter...

There was a commotion at the front door below. Ryder glanced at Braxton, turned, and hurried downstairs.

The police at the entry were speaking with two people. One a young man, perhaps thirty, dignified-looking in a business suit. He had dark hair that had been pushed back in his nervousness, soft brown eyes, and a medium build.

The woman was older, thin, and straight-backed, with gray hair queued at her nape. Ryder knew them. He'd met them at Lena's wedding. Justin Marceau, Anthony Marceau's second cousin, and Gail Reeves, the head housekeeper.

"Ryder!" Justin said. "Oh, my God, I saw the ambulance—"

"Where's the baby? What's happened?" Gail demanded. "I'm trying to tell these buffoons I work here. I manage the house. Lena! Where is Lena? Where is the baby?"

"Lena is dead. The baby is safe," Ryder said quietly. "Where have you been?" he asked Gail, looking at Justin to add, "And what are you doing here?"

Both burst into tears. Amidst it all, they learned it had been Gail's afternoon off. No, they hadn't been at the house earlier. Justin had come now because he'd heard that a few members of the board were coming by to explain a hike in the price of one of the drugs the company manufactured.

Ryder wondered if the display of tears was real. Justin was a Marceau...

But the estate and the company had been left to the baby, or rather her legal guardian, to watch over all until she was of age.

He didn't want to see Lena again, not even as she was, an angel. He had touched her...

And nothing.

Ryder left the Marceau mansion. He'd go see Lena's sister, Stephanie Harrow, as soon as he could. As well as his cousin's friend, Vicki, who had little Annette.

How that baby loved her mother. And how Lena had doted on her beloved child.

No.

No matter what anyone said, Lena wouldn't have left her baby.

He hesitated as he reached the SUV he borrowed from the local FBI agency when he was in the city.

Another car had just arrived. It was expensive, a Mercedes he noted. Three men emerged. The one who appeared to be the leader was in a gray suit that fit well with his white hair and well-groomed beard and mustache. The man behind him was tall and thin, probably in his early forties, wearing a blue suit.

The last man was young. He wore a sweatsuit, and his hair was damp. It looked as if he'd been pulled from the gym.

Ryder knew who they were. Barton Quincy, Larry Swenson, and Harry Miller. The three sat on the Marceau company's board of directors with Lena's late husband. Ryder had seen them briefly four years ago when his cousin, Lena, married Anthony Marceau.

One of you is a murderer! he thought. *One of you on the board of directors, or...*

Gail Reeves? The housekeeper?

Why?

Or Justin—also a board member—who was still weeping over Lena's death?

Ryder didn't know. All he knew was that his cousin had not committed suicide.

Braxton came to the front door to meet the first man, Barton Quincy, who seemed upset and then visibly angry. But Braxton was firm, not letting them enter the house.

The group departed in a huff. The older man in the gray suit paused as he reached the chauffeur-driven car, then turned to stare at the house.

Ryder could read the signs already. The medical examiner was going to declare Lena's death a suicide.

He would prove that it hadn't been.

Against the odds, he would prove it. Somehow.

And it wouldn't matter how long it took. Because her death would haunt him for as long as he lived.

Chapter 1

August

"Casey, I don't understand what you're looking for," Lauren Howard said. She stood and stared down a path of gothic tombs, all encased in the weeds and decay of the hundreds of years the cemetery had existed.

She was a pretty girl with dark hair, green eyes, and dusky skin. Clad in a colorful halter dress, she seemed at odds with the cemetery, even in the bright light of the rising sun.

"Looking for? Why, of course. It is Casey, medium extraordinaire. She seeks...yes! She seeks the walking dead," Jared Vincent told Lauren.

He grotesquely lifted his arms and stumbled forward, pretending to be a zombie. Jared was tall and lanky with soft brown hair that fell around his face. He made a strange-looking revenant.

Casey Nicholson sighed, then shook her head and smiled at her business partners.

This place was new to her friends. The graveyard was small compared to some of the other city cemeteries, which had become beautiful, haunted tourist attractions. There was only a small chapel in this one. It was built with funds raised by a priest through the Marceau family, who were grateful when a child made it through the yellow fever epidemic of 1853.

Casey had always loved the beauty of the city's cemeteries. And while St. Louis #1—and St. Louis #2 and #3—were the most often visited by tourists, along with Lafayette Cemetery in the Garden District, St. Mary of Light Chapel and Cemetery was small, old, off the beaten path, and seldom visited.

It was still charming. Haunting, eerie, and sad in its decaying beauty.

"Who runs this place? The chapel was deconsecrated, right?" Lauren asked.

"Yes, I believe so," Casey said. "I think it's taken care of by the Marceau Foundation. Marceau money was used to create it. The family was Catholic and had been praying to the Virgin Mary. When the sick little girl in their family survived, they built the chapel and started the cemetery. They had the land for one, and..."

She stood and pointed across the cemetery. "The family mansion still stands just over there."

Casey wasn't sure who was running the company anymore. An elder family member had died, then the supposed heir apparent, and then his wife. But there were still members of the extended family all over the country. And the corporation had a board of directors. Someone would be claiming the corporation—and the money.

The money meant nothing in Casey's mind. Tragedy had struck the family. Including a young parent, so devastated by grief that she had taken her life.

Casey had met Lena Marceau a few times when she came into the shop. She had been sweet and unassuming. Casey hadn't even known it was her until she'd been given the woman's credit card for payment.

"And so, here we are. Hanging around the dead on a beautiful morning. You know, Casey, I love the shop. But, honestly, couldn't we have gotten something out of a really cool voodoo congregation or the like?"

"Jennie Sanders is coming today. She's my best client. And she feels that something from this cemetery is haunting her. I have to know what it's like in person," Casey said.

"Maybe it's because I grew up here, but when you've seen one cool and haunted *city of the dead*, you've seen them all," Jared said.

"Jaded," Lauren accused.

"The funerary art is similar but different," Casey nodded towards a statue.

"Right! Enjoy the art. It is beautiful," Lauren said.

"And rotting," Jared noted. He must have noticed how they both stared at him and then added, "Hey, I'm here, right?"

New Orleans was famous for its atmospheric cemeteries, but Casey, Lauren, and Jared had been born and raised in New Orleans. The sometimes-eerie *cities of the dead* as the cemeteries were often called, were something they had grown up with. Casey's parents had lived across Rampart Street in the French Quarter, and she had been just a block or so from St. Louis #1 most of her life.

This wasn't one of the St. Louis cemeteries, though, and it was definitely off the beaten tourist track.

"Guys, I need to get a feel for this place. Like I said, Jennie Sanders is coming by the shop this morning for another reading, and I want to at least...well, to be able to say something," Casey explained.

"You aren't really a medium," Lauren reminded her. "And Jennie Sanders spends a lot of time on Bourbon Street and loves a few places on Frenchman Street. Not to mention, she loves to meet up with old friends at the bars on Decatur. She sees lots of *spirits*."

"That's right. You're not a medium," Jared noted.

"I never claimed to be."

"You're a psychologist," he added.

"Right. One who couldn't find work after college." Casey tried to hide her irritation with her friends. "And, again, I call myself a *reader*. I don't claim to be a medium. Come on! The place is called *A Beautiful Mind*," she added. "Art, music, and a sense of helping people solve their problems."

"You know, think about it. We could liven things up. You could call yourself a medium," Lauren said excitedly. "Oh, imagine. I could costume you in gypsy skirts and do a fantastic headpiece for you. We could stand on the street, and Jared could play his guitar, and we'd all sing *Lady Marmalade*. Imagine! We'd draw the tourists in."

Casey groaned—loudly. "Guys, give me a break. I just read the signs. And it works out fine. No singing on the street. Let's be happy, huh? Come on, you two. It's a miracle I found the shop and that we scraped up the money to buy it."

Jared elbowed Lauren, nodding in acknowledgement to Casey. "And, seriously, she's the best fake medium in the city because she *is* a psychologist. She tries to tell people to look at a situation and do the right thing."

"Nice, thank you." Casey grinned. "I'll take that."

She decided not to mention that none of them had received degrees that would help them much in the real world. Lauren had been an art major, and Jared had a degree in music— they both had fine arts degrees.

Lauren and Jared were both exceptionally talented, in Casey's mind, but they all survived because of the shop.

Jared often played his guitar outside. Sometimes, Lauren and Casey joined him, and they had fun—until someone went into the shop, and Jared had to finish up alone.

They sold Lauren's sketches and paintings and jewelry creations, along with tee shirts, and specially created NOLA souvenirs.

Casey glanced at her watch. New Orleans didn't tend to be an early city. They never opened the doors to the shop until ten, but it was almost ten now.

"Hey, look." Lauren pointed. "There. That tomb is freshly sealed."

Casey saw that the entrance to one of the more spectacular family mausoleums *had* been freshly sealed.

"Maybe they were actually getting ready to repair this place," Jared wondered. "My brother came through here once when one of the *oven* doors was cracked. Said there were bones sticking out. I did hear the upkeep of the St. Louis cemeteries and Lafayette has gotten a lot better in our lifetimes—though maybe Lafayette was kept up all the time. You said you think the Marceau Foundation runs this place?"

"I think so, with the church managing the daily operations. But Marceau Industries Incorporated helps too," Lauren said.

"Rich people there. But here...I mean, I don't know why the family doesn't donate the cemetery to a historical society or something of the like. It's all falling apart," Jared said.

They stopped and stared at the tomb. It was both Gothic and Victorian in style and resembled a small colonial mansion with arches and gargoyles with a winged angel cradling a cross atop the roof of the old structure.

Stone and metal plaques mentioned the names of those interred, from the first family member to the latest.

"Oh, my God," Lauren breathed.

"You're right. Look. This is the Marceau family mausoleum," Casey said.

"Someone was just interred here. Lena Marceau," Jared added. He whispered as if afraid he might wake the sleeping dead within the tomb. "Man, we should have thought of that."

"Lena Marceau. Of course," Casey murmured, thinking it odd that she had just been thinking about the woman. She had, of course, read about the young woman's death. Her sister had found her, looking as if she were merely asleep. The investigation was leaning toward suicide.

Lena's husband had died just the year before. It was presumed that she had never gotten over his death.

The facts were heartbreaking.

"This is so, so sad," Casey said softly, feeling the truth of her words.

"You knew her?" Jared asked.

"She came into the shop a few times. She was nice. She had a great smile, and was fun. She came in with her daughter. The baby is so beautiful. When we decided to come here, I had nearly forgotten all about...what happened. Though I figured the family had a really grand mausoleum in one of the major cemeteries by now."

"Sad, yes. And selfish." Lauren frowned and looked perplexed. "She had a two-year-old baby depending on her. If her sister hadn't arrived early, the baby might have...well, she might have gotten seriously hurt. You don't commit suicide when you have a two-year-old."

"Maybe she didn't commit suicide," Casey murmured.

"It was all over the news and in the papers," Lauren said. "She was alone. There was no evidence of a break-in. I heard there was supposed to be a board meeting at the mansion later that day, but she locked the baby in her supposedly childproof room for a nap and took enough pills to kill an elephant. What else could it have been but suicide? She overtook prescription drugs. There was no sign of violence. I guess I should have figured she'd be buried here. I remember once thinking the board for Marceau Industries Incorporated must be a bunch of really mean old men. They were probably so horrible to her, she couldn't stand it anymore. Maybe she even figured the baby would be better off if she was dead. She was alone with all those monsters. Her husband...yeah. Look. His name is here. He was interred here, too. I don't know why I didn't think anybody was buried here any longer."

"People who commit suicide usually suffer from terrible depression and believe others will be better off without them," Casey said. "And the family owns the place...I wasn't thinking either. I imagined she might be buried at Lafayette Cemetery. But, obviously, the family still has this beautiful mausoleum, so...it makes sense she'd be interred here."

"Weird. I think there are a few more of these smaller cemeteries that still aren't part of the major foundation that looks out for most of the historic cemeteries in the city," Jared said. "But nothing this size. Even if it seems tiny next to the St. Louis cemeteries or those in Metairie—some of which are huge. Anyway...it's good we came." He was trying to lighten the mood, Casey knew. "We all learned something we didn't know and came to a place we've never been—in the city we grew up in." He looked at Casey and likely saw the expression on her face. "Hey, it's okay."

She smiled. She didn't want to describe the sadness she felt for someone she had barely known.

"Now we know there was a recent interment. This is good," Jared said earnestly. "So, when our *spirited* lady comes in, you'll know how to direct her concerns."

"It just feels odd. I...I don't mean to be irreverent. We should have thought of it before. I mean, Lena Marceau died. As you said, it was all over the news," Casey murmured.

"Again, we didn't know she'd been interred here. Our client thinks she saw a ghost, and now Casey will know who the spirit was," Jared said and winked.

Casey glanced at her watch again, disturbed that they were making light of such a tragic death. People died every day, of course, but it was just that...Lena Marceau had left a baby behind. And her husband had died just the year before.

It didn't seem fair or right. And it didn't seem...plausible. Trying to think back, Casey thought Lena Marceau had been in the shop right before Mardi Gras.

"Why don't you two go ahead and get the shop opened? I just want to wander for a few more minutes," she said.

"You shouldn't do that. The family wasn't always known for being kind. Maybe the ghost is evil," Jared teased. "I think they practiced weird voodoo!"

Casey sighed patiently. "Jared."

"Oh, Casey, I'm sorry. I didn't realize...I'm sorry. It was tragic. No more cemeteries. We're next door to a voodoo shop, guys, with the nicest priestess in the world. Voodoo is not weird or creepy. Not real voodoo anyway. What Papa Doc did in Haiti was a perversion, just like Hollywood makes it all out to be. Our voodoo priestess is sweet and wonderful. Let's do stuff with her when you need to find some mojo to feed to a client," Jared said.

"Hey," Lauren added lightly, "you've left coins at Marie Laveau's tomb," she said as a reminder.

"Because it's the thing to do. Go. Please. You two are driving me crazy!"

"We're going, we're going. But don't blame us if the ghost of an evil voodoo priest gets his talons in you," Jared said.

"I promise you, I won't."

Casey watched them leave, laughing together as they headed down the main gravel path of the little cemetery.

She studied the tomb again. There might have been recent interments, but there were still vines growing all over the structure, and weeds had proliferated at the base.

Someone had left flowers at the iron gate of the tomb. Casey bent down for a closer look. The flowers had been there for maybe a day. There was a note with them. Simple.

It read: *Love you so much.*

Casey felt something on her shoulder and turned, startled and angry, thinking that Lauren or Jared had doubled back to tease her.

But it wasn't Lauren.

Or Jared.

A young woman stood there, blonde and beautiful with striking blue eyes.

Casey blinked. She had seen the woman before.

It was Lena Marceau.

Not dead at all? Or...

Then the woman spoke softly, and her words were almost like a rustle, her hand nothing more than air upon Casey's shoulder.

"You're not real!" Casey gasped.

She was suddenly angry.

They had done this to her—Jared and Lauren. They had made her feel as if the place were creepy and eerie, that spirits could roam the Earth.

It couldn't be happening. It wasn't even night. It was day, and a bright and beautiful one. The sun shone brightly...

Showing her a strange translucence in the woman before her.

"Well, yes. And no," the specter said.

"I'm not seeing you!" Casey protested.

"But you do see me," the apparition argued.

No, no, no, no, no!

Casey wasn't sure what happened next.

The world suddenly went dark.

She must have...passed out.

She'd never fainted in her life. But she was suddenly lying atop the step to the tomb, and she still wasn't alone.

The figure remained. The young blonde woman who was...who *had been*...Lena Marceau. The apparition. The figment of her imagination. The...

Here Casey was, with her psychology degree, going stark raving mad.

"Please!" the woman implored. "Please, please. I'm so sorry. But I need your help! Not for me, it's far too late for that, but please...my sister and my baby are out there."

Darkness seemed to surround Casey again, enveloping her in a stygian embrace.

How crazy...

Then, nothing.

* * * *

Ryder sat at his desk at Krewe headquarters in Virginia, concentrating on the last of his paperwork for the case he and Axel Tiger had just finished up in Colorado.

He hit the last letter key to finish his work and sat back.

He'd been glad to head to Colorado and work with Axel. His level of frustration had been high. The autopsy on his cousin had shown nothing the M.E. hadn't already suspected: an overdose of prescription drugs.

He'd spent a week with his cousin Stephanie, working with her and old Elijah's superb lawyer to make sure she had solid protection at the mansion and to ensure that the Marceau inheritance had been sewn up for little Annette.

He'd also researched the board, the family, and any others who might have had access to Lena and her home at the time of his cousin's death.

Someone had to have been involved.

He just didn't know who.

But he'd been spinning his wheels in New Orleans.

Bottom line, he knew that he had to find out who wanted control of the Marceau inheritance enough to kill.

Cunningly, and several times over.

And now...

Well, a baby was theoretically in charge.

Five people—all of whom he had seen on the day Lena died—might be involved. He had thought so then, and he still thought so.

People who were close to the day-to-day workings of the Marceau home and business—Gail Reeves, the housekeeper, who'd happened to have an afternoon off. Barton Quincy, director of operations at Marceau

Industries Incorporated. Larry Swenson, Barton's second in command. Harry Miller, sales director. And Justin Marceau, another great-grandson, who had grown up in Baltimore, Maryland, but had taken his place on the board of directors.

Justin wasn't always in the city, but he had been in New Orleans on the day Lena died. And after the baby, Justin was next in line to inherit. Could Justin be involved? Or was he in danger just as the others had been because his last name was Marceau?

But even Ryder couldn't make sense of the fact that there had been no defensive wounds on Lena's body. There had been no alcohol by her side, either. Nothing to indicate that her mind hadn't been right, other than what everyone thought to be obvious depression enough to bring on suicide. There also hadn't been evidence that anyone had forced her to take the pills.

Ryder had seen video of the immediate property. He and Stephanie had gone over it together. On the feed, he saw Lena, holding little baby Annette and waving goodbye as Gail Reeves headed out. They never saw the housekeeper return.

At the estimated time of Lena's death, there was a mysterious blackout in the video.

Ryder had stayed in the city for two weeks, but a snag in a video reel—no matter how timely and mysterious—hadn't been enough for anyone but him to call Lena's death a murder. He knew Braxton had even pursued the matter with his superiors at the NOPD.

Braxton had let him watch as he interviewed Gail Reeves, Barton Quincy, Larry Swenson, Harry Miller, and even Justin Marceau. They'd all been brought in not as suspects, but in hopes they could give the police some indication of what might have happened with Lena. They all came in willingly, eager to help.

Or so they said.

And then...

Not even Jackson Crow, the field director for the Krewe, had managed to find a reason to home in on the investigation.

Eventually, Jackson had assured Ryder that they would pursue it further. But that meant a lot of research. Thankfully, Jackson had cooled Ryder down enough to work another case while the tech experts, Angela's incredibly talented group of *paper chasers,* had delved into the paper and digital trails.

But there had been a bright spot in it all. Adam Harrison, the assistant director over all of the Krewe and their magnanimous founder, had agreed with Ryder and Jackson that it was all far too suspicious.

A happily married man—Lena's husband, Anthony—had managed to fall off the roof of a building in the Central Business District after visiting a bank branch there when there was another branch just down the street from his home. And, equally suspicious, a young woman who adored her child and appeared to be in fine health committing suicide.

Not to mention the fact that a fortune was at stake.

The Krewe would not give up, but it was the kind of case where many people needed to be investigated, and a great deal of material needed to be reviewed.

Though none were better at that kind of investigation than Angela's paper chasers.

Jackson had suggested that Ryder take on the case in Colorado with Axel while he let Angela and the tech crew perform research on the people and events surrounding the murders.

Ryder couldn't forget seeing Lena lying there like an angel. Nor the hurt in Stephanie's eyes. Or the baby's confused tears and frustration. Annette was too young to understand what had happened.

It had been heartbreaking to hear the baby crying for her mother.

Thankfully, Annette loved her Aunt Stephanie.

Jackson had been right. Ryder was better when working a case. Right now, his head pounded. He pressed his temples between his palms.

And then...

Timing couldn't have been better. He gritted his teeth against the pain and hit *Send* on his latest report just when a tap sounded at his door.

Angela. She had been with Jackson when the Krewe first came together on a case in New Orleans. They were now married and the parents of an adopted ten-year-old boy and a baby girl. She was a beautiful blonde woman who somehow managed it all—parenting and working and answering the phone at odd hours.

"Hello," he said, looking at her hopefully. "Did you find anything?"

She smiled. "I do have something," she told him. "Not much, but something. Did you ever hear of or do you know anything about a man named William Marley?"

"William Marley...yes. Or no. I never knew him, but when I was studying some company papers with Stephanie, his name was mentioned. He was sixty-six, still working on the board, close to Elijah and Anthony Marceau, when he died of a heart attack."

Angela nodded. "I pulled his medical records. He didn't have a heart condition, but he did die in a hospital, and there was no autopsy."

"If he died in a hospital—"

"I don't believe the doctors were at fault. The ambulance got him to the doors of the hospital, but he died being transferred from the rescue vehicle to the emergency room. It was evident he had died of a heart attack. He was sent to the morgue but was quickly transferred to the Devereaux funeral home in New Orleans." She was quiet for a minute. "Lena Marceau arranged for his burial. She was close with William Marley, like she was with Elijah and Anthony."

"Can we dig him up?"

Angela sighed. "Ryder. You grew up in Kenner. William Marley was interred in the Marceau family mausoleum. And he died before Anthony. If you understand New Orleans, which you must..."

"A year and a day," Ryder murmured. That was the time it took for the Louisiana sun to basically cremate a body. "Still, Angela. I was at a forensic workshop as a cop. Cremains can leave clues. The year and a day simply means the body has deteriorated enough to be pushed into a holding cell at the end of the vault to allow for another interment. There might be something in the bones or the ash. I'm not an M.E. or even a tech geek, but I believe certain things—"

"Can be derived from bone and ash. There might be. But we're going to need permission to open the vault."

"We can get that. That will be the easy part. And if we find something in the bones or the ash, they'll have to reopen the case."

Angela smiled at him. "It's better than that. William Marley was on a trip to play at the casino in Biloxi. He died right over the state line in Mississippi. If we find anything, we can claim the case ourselves."

Ryder hopped up and rushed over to her, crushing her to him and twirling her around. He did so just as Jackson Crow happened to come down the hallway.

"What?" Jackson asked, a curious look in his eyes and a smile on his face.

"Your wife is brilliant!" Ryder told him.

"I know that," Jackson said. "Ah. She told you what she found."

"She did." Ryder winced. He had the best job in the world, and he never wanted to lose it. It was the only kind of work that could keep a man like him sane—and, hopefully, create a better world by bringing justice to those robbed of life and bringing closure to the ones left behind.

But Lena's death would haunt him to his dying day.

He'd discovered that he could talk to the dead when he was young.

He'd been put in therapy, of course.

So he'd learned not to mention it to others.

Until he heard about the Krewe of Hunters.

He'd gone to Lena's autopsy. He'd attended the funeral. He'd prowled the Marceau mansion.

But he hadn't found any remnant of her spirit—and he'd searched.

"Jackson, I'd like—"

"To go back to New Orleans. Go. You'll have to book a commercial flight; we have a team heading out to San Diego with the jet."

"Commercial is fine. I'm just a visitor. Stephanie can order the opening of the vault, and Braxton and his people are good; they just had nowhere else to go in their investigation. And I understand how others think Lena's death was a suicide. But if—"

"If we can prove William Marley was helped into his heart attack, we can take over the case," Angela finished for him.

"Book your flight," Jackson told him.

"I already booked him one," Angela said. She glanced at her watch. "Better move. Your plane leaves in three hours."

"I'll be on it," Ryder assured her.

"And keep in touch. We're always here—or somewhere—if you need us."

"Will do," Ryder promised.

He picked up his phone. He had to tell Stephanie that he was on his way and warn her what he needed to do.

Investigate a corpse.

She wasn't going to be happy.

But Stephanie wanted to live. And she wanted to protect the baby at all costs.

She would do what was necessary.

Even if they had a fight on their hands.

Chapter 2

It was a given.

Summer in New Orleans was hot. The dead heat of July and August hung on into the early weeks of September, and just stepping outside was like taking a bath in sweat. Thankfully, the air-conditioning in the shop worked well.

It wasn't that it was any different than usual. Not really. It was hot every year, and they complained every year. And then fall and winter finally arrived, and the temperatures were beautiful. But the fourplex where Casey lived had a lovely pool in back, and she was currently dreaming of jumping into it. It was even part of a screened-in patio so it kept the mosquitoes to a minimum.

But Jennie Sanders was in the shop again. And even if she weren't, it was Wednesday—one of Casey's nights to close.

Casey could dream about the cool splash of the pool all she wanted. Instead, she sat across from Jennie at a table in her room in the back of the shop, staring at tea leaves.

"What do you see?" Jennie asked anxiously.

What do I see, what do I see?

Tea leaves! Casey thought.

Jennie visited once a week and was a wonderful customer, buying items in the shop every time she came for a reading.

And Jared was right. The shop did well, but what Casey did most of the time was be the best listener she could—practicing psychology. While Casey knew that she was a total sham as a medium, she was equally convinced there was something unusual in Jennie Sanders. Jennie had a sixth sense, and her visits with Casey helped her recognize it in herself and deal with life's little difficulties more easily.

Jennie was in her late forties and had grown children. Her husband, a retired professor, was an indulgent man, and her children were off living and working in Atlanta. She made trips to see her grandchildren, but other than that, she had time on her hands. She was an attractive woman who kept fit and was as regular about attending her beauty salon and going to the gym as she was about visiting Casey.

"From what I'm seeing," Casey said, "if you drive and are careful, a trip to Atlanta to see the grandkids would be rewarding for you. They love you and miss you very much. Oh, and your daughter-in-law, Mike's wife, loves it when you come. It gives her more time to work on her macramé projects."

"Oh, thank you! That's what I felt, but...of course, I'll spend time with Mike and Sheila, and I'll spend time with Virginia and Al, too. And when I'm there, they get together more often."

"I don't think you need to worry. Your children will remain close to one another."

Casey had met them both. They'd come into the shop with Jennie a few times. Mike loved Lauren's artwork, and Virginia suggested bizarre songs for Jared to play on the street. Usually, Jared played a game of *Name that Tune!* or thought of ridiculous melodies and lyrics to go with whatever she challenged him with. It was hysterical.

Jennie had nice children who loved her. Casey didn't need tea leaves to know that.

"Great! Then I won't see you for a few weeks," Jennie said, getting up. "I'll miss you. I love coming in here—"

"I'm sure I'll be here when you get back," Casey said, rising and leading them both out to the main area of the shop.

"Unless," Jennie said dramatically, "a tall, dark, and dangerously handsome stranger appears and sweeps you off your feet and takes you far, far away. Honestly, I don't know how that hasn't happened yet. Sweetheart, you are lovely. So sweet and kind. I mean, I guess that doesn't equal sex appeal, but you're gorgeous, too. Hair like a blackbird, eyes like...something really blue."

"Luscious locks like a raven's wing, eyes like the sky at sweetest morning's dew!" Jared supplied, grinning at them both from behind the counter.

"Well, thank you both," Casey said. "Jennie, have a great trip. We'll hear all about it when you come back."

"Oh! I need to buy a few things. I'm going to take some of the latest watercolors Lauren has on display," Jennie said. "And I will be gone for a bit, so I'd love for Jared to give me a sendoff. With you lovely ladies, if you don't mind."

"I have just the thing," Jared said, grabbing his guitar. "John Denver, *Leaving on a Jet Plane*," he said.

He played. Casey and Lauren had done the song with him dozens of times before. It was always fun, falling into the harmony part, and Casey realized she was smiling when they finished.

"How was that?" Jared asked Jennie.

"Superb! Except I'm driving," Jennie said.

Jared grinned and burst into a rendition of the Beatles' tune, *Baby, You Can Drive My Car*.

He finished the song, and the older woman clapped. Lauren got the canvases that their customer wanted down from their hooks and wrapped them, listening as Jennie chatted all the while.

When Jennie left, Casey wandered toward the door and the street, wishing *she* could leave. But the shop had been her idea and was her baby. And given where they were located in the French Quarter on St. Anne Street, staying open until at least ten was par for the course and necessary to stay in business.

Casey had suggested that they alternate working the late shifts. She just wished this was her night to go home early.

Lauren and Jared had gone to LSU with her. They were truly close friends, and if she had begged one of them to take her place, they would have done so. But she knew they planned on heading to Frenchman Street to see a band that one of Jared's old frat brothers had formed.

She'd just look out the window.

But Jennie came back, obviously determined to speak to her again.

"Have you been back to the cemetery where the Marceau mausoleum is?" Jennie asked in a soft voice.

"No, I haven't. I'm sorry, Jennie." She tried not to let the woman see how just the mention of the place gave her shivers.

"You need to go back. I told you, my dream was vivid. There was a woman there, sobbing. And I don't know if she was dead or alive, but she clearly needs help. I mean, if she *is* dead, then you're the person to go."

A sobbing woman.

Yes. If her crazy break with reality had any substance, the sobbing woman was Lena Marceau. And yet...

No. Never again. Casey still didn't know what she'd seen or imagined that day. She only knew that she had awakened in an ambulance with doctors desperately trying to figure what had caused a healthy twenty-four-year-old woman to pass out in a cemetery.

Heatstroke had been the verdict—and a common one. It had occurred in the middle of the dead of summer, after all.

"Jennie, the dead are beyond our earthly help. But I can find someone with the church or talk to someone at Marceau Industries Incorporated. Make sure they look through the cemetery and see that all is well there. I believe they're taking better care of it these days. I heard restoring her husband's family mausoleum had meant something to Lena Marceau. And her sister, Stephanie, is now guardian to Lena's little girl, Annette. She's been keeping up with her sister's intentions. So, all should be well."

"I still think you should go," Jennie said. "You have such a way. Well, you do what you can, and I'll call you with any more dreams."

Casey forced a smile. "You do that," she said.

At last, Jennie was gone again. Casey walked back into the center of the shop. Jared was back behind the counter, and Lauren was adjusting some framed work on the walls.

"Hey, you two better get going," Casey said, glancing at her watch. "Jennie stayed late. It's after six."

"The band doesn't start until eight," Jared told her. "We're good. But, Lauren, let's get out of here. I want to stop and get something to eat."

"Where?"

"I don't know. We'll head over there and wander. Okay?"

"Sounds good to me."

The two didn't actually leave for another few minutes. Lauren was intent on getting everything on the wall straight and precise, and Jared greeted two new customers who came in and set them up for a reading the next week.

When they left, Casey wished she'd set the shop's closing hours earlier than she had. Because of all the diners out in the area and the many other shops that stayed open late, they closed at ten.

Customers came and went. For the most part, they were nice. People tended to like tarot cards because so many of the decks were so artistic and beautiful, and it was fun to discover that a so-called bad card might not be bad at all, depending on where it fell.

Casey had a nice time with a group of college kids that came in, explaining a few of the cards.

Decks were also reasonably priced, and something people could afford.

A man in his early forties came in while the girls were still there. He spoke to Casey casually about her readings and said he was thinking about tea leaves because they fascinated him. He bought one of Lauren's prints and said he'd be back to schedule a reading.

Darkness fell.

An older man came in. He looked a bit like a well-groomed Santa. He didn't seem the type concerned with a reading, but he asked her about tea leaves and the tarot, then grinned and asked her about her crystal ball.

"The only one we have is in the statue over there," she told him. "Everything I do is learned from books, sir, and I haven't found one to explain what I'd be seeing in a crystal ball. Except, well, they are pretty."

"They are."

He was pleasant and curious and asked her if she'd been a music major. She told him it was psychology, and that seemed to amuse him. He said it clearly explained the shop.

After that, he bought a few of their tee shirts, thanked her, and left.

It was almost ten, and she sank into one of the comfortable chairs by the small coffee and tea station they had in the far corner. Most of Lauren's work could be seen from that vantage point. It was a nice little nook where they had the table with a pod machine and plush chairs covered in a very dark crimson material that added to the masks and art and other décor in the shop.

Casey closed her eyes. The bell would ring when someone came in.

The bell didn't ring. But when she opened her eyes, someone was facing her.

Lena Marceau.

She opened her mouth, but a scream didn't come.

"Please, please, don't pass out on me again!" Lena—or the ghost or specter of the woman—said. "I'm so sorry! But you're a medium. You should have known I might be here."

Casey didn't pass out. Maybe she was too frozen to do so. All she could do was reply with, "I'm not a medium."

"But—"

"I read tea leaves and tarot cards. I don't even have a crystal ball."

She was talking—and talking out loud. To a ghost. But no matter how she blinked, the apparition didn't go away.

Lena spoke again. "Look, I don't understand any of this, and I'm so sorry. I have no choice. You must help me! They're going to kill my sister and my baby."

Casey realized that she was breathing heavily. She pinched herself—it was what was done in situations like these, right?

The pinch hurt.

But Lena Marceau still sat before her.

"I've tried to reach my sister. I've tried so hard. But I...well, I don't know how any of this works. By the time I came to myself—as a spirit or whatever—the funeral was over, and people had gone. My sister comes to the cemetery, but she doesn't see me. I know she senses something is wrong, though. And, oh, Lord! Ryder was there. Ryder is with the FBI, but he was gone by the time I realized I had to try to reach someone. And this isn't easy. I go by some people, and they shiver. And I have tried voodoo shops and magic shops and churches. I really thought you would see me—and accept me. I have met a few others like me, and they told me I needed to find the right person. That some people can see us. Not many, but they do exist. Please, please, you have to help me!"

Was Lena—or Lena's spirit—really there? Or was Casey conversing with herself?

There was no reason for her to have a psychotic break. She'd had no trauma in her life. She had good friends, a great home, and super parents who now lived in Arizona but came to see her regularly and loved her very much. Both were well.

"Please!" the ghost said.

"Lena, I bought this shop because I was a psychology major. When I got out of college, the jobs I was offered would have barely paid back my student loans. I grew up here, and I have been in this type of shop before, and I know...well, I've studied people. I've studied books on the tarot. When I say I read cards, I just talk about what the books say, along with what I believe the client is looking for or needs. I don't have any special abilities—"

"But you're talking to me."

Casey let out a soft sigh.

"Yes. Apparently, I've gone crazy."

"No, no. You're not crazy. I'm here. Well, I'm not *physically* here, but... Please, help me!"

"How? You keep talking about *they*. Who are they? What—what happened?" She took a deep breath. "I'm guessing you didn't kill yourself.

I never thought it made any sense, but there was something of an investigation. An autopsy. You didn't fight with anyone. You just took the pills. What happened, *who* is involved?"

"I don't know exactly. I just know someone in that wretched company Elijah left Anthony and me, killed us both."

"Lena. First, I'm still trying to decide if there's been a trauma in my life I didn't realize that caused a psychotic break, or if...if it's possible you're here. But after that, there's still a serious problem. I can't just go to the police and tell them your ghost told me you were murdered!"

Lena sat back, looking around the store. "I always loved this place."

"Thank you. Lena—"

"You need to go to my sister and warn her."

"And your sister is not going to hit me or laugh me off the doorstep?"

"Stephanie won't hit you. She's nice."

"But she will think I'm a crazy person and laugh me off the doorstep," Casey said.

"We have to do something," Lena whispered.

"Lena, how can it be you don't know what happened to you?"

The beautiful blonde ghost leaned back in Casey's chair and looked up at the ceiling, shaking her head. "I don't know."

"How can you not know?"

She shook her head again. "He—I'm sure it was a *he*—didn't want me to know who he was. Maybe he's a believer in the dead coming back to life, or he wasn't sure if there were cameras in the house. We never had cameras in the house. I was in my bedroom when a masked person broke in, holding the baby—Annette had been taking a nap in her room—and a knife. I—I bargained with him. Said I'd take the pills. I'd make it look like a suicide. But told him he had to let me lock the baby in her room first. Said he couldn't touch her." Her ghostly fists clenched. "I needed to say goodbye," she whispered.

The thought of making such a decision, of all that it cost Lena, broke Casey's heart.

"Only my sister and I know the code to that door, and I knew Stephanie was coming over within the hour. It wasn't ideal, but the room was babyproofed, secure, and it was the only thing I could think to do." She paused for a minute. "At least I saved Annette. He wanted to kill us both. I told him I'd fight tooth and nail, and everyone would know we'd been murdered. So, I bargained for her life."

"I'm so sorry," Casey whispered.

Lena shrugged. "Anthony inherited the house, you know. No one had lived in it for a while, and...the reason Elijah left him the company was because Anthony didn't really want it. He didn't care about the money—he was an artist. A good one. But he'd loved Elijah since he was a little boy, and Elijah loved him. When it all came up about five years ago, I said, 'Sure, we'll live in your old family house, and we'll try to do good things.' I damned us both with that."

"You're not damned."

"No, I don't think so. And I've heard people move on when...when they're ready. When the time comes. Into a beautiful light. But the thing is, Anthony and I...we're both dead," Lena said bitterly. "I wouldn't care so much, except..."

"You're worried about Annette."

"And my sister. Casey, don't you see? They'll kill her and Annette."

"Okay, so a man was there with a knife. You don't know who."

"He wore black—black pants, black hoodie, black ski mask...completely covered. And I never got close to him. I couldn't recognize a smell or anything like that. I'm not even sure about the color of his eyes because I think he was wearing weird costume contact lenses. I don't know who he was. I beg you, help me. At least get to Stephanie and warn her that she's in danger. And tell her that...he wanted to kill the baby when he killed me."

This can't be real.

But Casey could see Lena sitting there. Maybe it was her own strange sense of guilt. Or the way she had felt at St. Mary of Light Cemetery while seeing the Marceau tomb.

"I don't know how much help I can give you," Casey said. "But—"

"But?"

"Of course, I'll help in any way I can. Tomorrow...I'll find a way to see your sister. I'll warn her that she's in danger. She'll probably tell me I'm a quack who owns a mystic shop and thinks she's got a direct phone line to the Underworld."

"Stephanie isn't stupid. I believe she knows she could be in danger. I need her to know just how much," Lena said.

Casey nodded. "Okay, I...I'll do my best."

* * * *

"You're back," Braxton said, forcing a weak smile as he greeted Ryder.

Ryder had told Braxton not to worry about picking him up at the airport. Said he could grab transportation himself.

But Braxton had insisted on coming, and he was here now, waiting for Ryder in the baggage claim section of Louis Armstrong International Airport.

"Yes, I'm back," Ryder said, shaking Braxton's hand. His old friend looked at him with skeptical worry. "Ryder, you know that—"

"I'm not going to be a pain," Ryder promised.

"But you're here because of the Marceau incident," Braxton said. "Ryder, it's over. The M.E. found nothing but an overdose of prescribed sedatives in her system."

"Don't forget, Lena Marceau was my cousin."

"Second cousin. Your mothers were cousins."

"I don't care what kind of cousin."

"But no suicide note was ever discovered. You're my friend. I tried. But the medical examiner, as you know, found nothing else," Braxton said, his tone miserable.

"Right," Ryder said. "And still, the Marceau fortune is in the hands of a two-year-old child. But I know when Elijah died, they discovered his will was extensive and detailed. Control went to Anthony, and then to Lena, and then from her to the baby, Annette, controlled by her legal guardian until she comes of age. And Stephanie Harrow is the baby's legal guardian now. Everything is hers, held in trust. And after her husband died, Lena saw to it that her sister was added to the corporation's board of directors."

"That can't sit well with the rest of the family and board members."

"There are five other people on that board, Braxton, including Justin Marceau."

"Oh, come on. You think that—"

"I do," Ryder interrupted, speaking firmly. But then he hesitated. "Stephanie called me last night. She was out with the baby and realized she was being followed. She didn't head back to the house but went straight to Bourbon Street."

"With a two-year-old child?"

"She knew there would be people there, plenty of witnesses. She found one of your officers and said he was a good guy. She asked him to see that she and the baby got home safely, and he did. Braxton, I'm just going to hang around and see what I can find out. Anthony and Lena dead within months of one another—by accident or suicide—and that starting a year after old Elijah passed on? I'm not knocking the NOLA police, you know that I'm not, but I believe that something more is going on. Come on, Braxton."

"Yes, but..." Braxton paused, shaking his head. "We've gotten word the FBI is disinterring a fellow who worked for the corporation—who conveniently died in Mississippi."

"Yes."

"But, Ryder—"

"If his heart attack was induced, then even you will have to admit it's starting to look suspicious."

"Induced? But a heart attack—"

"William didn't have a heart condition."

"But a heart attack—"

"*Can* be induced."

Braxton sighed and shook his head.

"Braxton, Jackson Crow obviously knows I'm here. I'm not official, again, no one has asked us in. And I'm not going to get in your way. But I'm going to be around for Stephanie, all right?"

"I just want you to be careful. We have a great relationship with the Krewe down here. Your Krewe of Hunters started up in NOLA, you know."

"I do know that," Ryder said. And he did. He knew the history of the Krewe. He'd wanted to be FBI for as long as he could remember. His father was a retired agent. When he heard about the Krewe—through rumor, mostly—he'd known what he wanted. He'd been accepted into the academy when he made a point of finding Jackson Crow, knowing when the man would be at his son's baseball game.

But Jackson had already known about Ryder. He'd wondered about that until he passed the academy and became Krewe.

Then, he'd learned that Jackson had heard about the strange case in Alexandria that Ryder had solved as a young police detective.

He'd longed to be a part of a group that understood him.

As it happened, the group had been watching *him*.

"So, officially, you're what? On vacation?" Braxton asked skeptically.

"You could say that."

Braxton groaned but picked up Ryder's bag and headed to the elevators for the parking garage. "As far as the NOPD goes, the case is closed. Lena has been interred, and life goes on. Where am I taking you?"

"The Marceau house," Ryder said.

"You're staying at the Marceau mansion?"

"The baby invited me."

"Hey!" Braxton protested.

"The baby owns the house. Stephanie is her legal guardian. I'm here because Stephanie is afraid. She is convinced that her sister was murdered, Braxton. Doesn't it worry you? Anthony and Lena, both dead? Another man possibly murdered, and Stephanie all that stands between that baby and her life?"

"No one could want to kill a baby. Hey!" he exclaimed at Ryder's look. "When Lena died, the baby was fine."

"Fine. Because she'd been locked in a room, and only Stephanie had the code to get in. I think Lena was worried after Anthony died. I mean, think about it. Why would Anthony mysteriously jump or fall off a building in the Central Business District? He had a beautiful wife, a gorgeous child, and he'd just inherited an empire."

Braxton was quiet for a moment. "His death was ruled accidental. And we're all watching, just so you know. We're not stupid down here. If you can prove the Marceau exec was murdered, you're taking over the case."

"*Taking over* is strong. I expect we'll be a team, or possibly form a task force."

Braxton shook his head. "Okay, well...are you going to invite me to tea?"

"You want tea?"

Braxton grinned. "Isn't that what rich people do? Sip tea and eat crumpets?"

"As long as I've known Stephanie, she's been a coffee girl. But if you want tea, I'll get you some tea. And crumpets."

"What is a crumpet?"

"Something baked," Ryder said. "I don't know. Let's just get there. And then..."

"Then what?"

"I'm going to pay a visit to the Marceau mausoleum."

"Think Lena will tell you what happened?" Braxton asked dryly.

"You never know," Ryder told him. "You just never know."

Chapter 3

Casey stood at the gate before the Marceau house—or mansion rather.

Esplanade Avenue in New Orleans hosted some fine homes. This one was especially beautiful, combining Colonial and Victorian styles with a perfectly manicured lawn and charming fountains on either side of the grand walk to the porch steps.

There was a call button, and she hit it and waited. A minute later, she heard a feminine voice say, "Hello, may I help you?"

"Miss Harrow?" Casey said.

She was ready to run. The woman would simply refuse to see her.

"Yes, this is Stephanie Harrow. How may I help you?"

"It's a private and personal matter," Casey said and winced.

She wished Lena Marceau's ghost would appear now. She'd stayed late at the store, talking in general, enthusiastic terms about Lauren's art pieces and smiling about Jared's talent with music, saying that she'd seen him outside the shop a few times, though he hadn't been there when she visited. He could go from doing Beethoven to Broadway to heavy metal in a matter of minutes.

"He is extremely talented," Casey had said. "He was with a group, but they were doing heavy metal almost exclusively, and he felt he was burning out his voice. He likes being a solo act or telling Lauren and I what to do. He was the music major, so we never argue."

Lena had also talked about her daughter, laughing and saying how they hadn't lied when they'd come up with the term *terrible twos*.

It had been past ten when Casey yawned and closed her eyes, leaning back in her seat.

When she opened her eyes and started to apologize for nodding off, Lena was no longer there.

And Casey was left to wonder again if her own mind was haunting her.

She had decided that she wasn't going to approach Stephanie Harrow and the Marceau house unless she saw Lena again. But that night, as tired as she was, she had trouble sleeping. She tossed and turned and feared that everything the ghost—real or imagined—had said might be true. She couldn't imagine anyone wanting to hurt a child.

But it had to be true. Her husband's death. And her death. To Casey, it was just...

Too convenient.

"I'm sorry, but who are you?" Stephanie asked over the intercom.

"My name is Casey Nicholson. I own a shop in the French Quarter. I...your sister was a friend of mine."

She was greeted with dead silence for so long, she almost turned away.

Then she heard the grinding of gears as the gate opened.

She walked through and up the walkway to the front porch. As she climbed the steps, the front doors—beautiful wood and etched glass—opened.

A woman walked out.

Stephanie Harrow was a few years older than Lena had been. Her hair was a darker shade of blond, cut short in a bob to frame her chin. She was an attractive woman, but her face seemed somehow marred by the sorrow she had faced.

"Come in," she told Casey.

"Thank you."

"Coffee?" Stephanie asked.

"I never turn down morning coffee," Casey told her.

"Then please, come on through to the kitchen. The parlor here...it's too big for me."

The parlor was big. But it was the entry with its sweeping staircase to the second floor in the center of the room that seemed to dominate the space.

"I used to love this place," Stephanie murmured. "Lena came down those stairs in her wedding dress, and it was spectacular. Now... Were you at the wedding?" she asked, frowning.

"No." Casey glanced down. "We met when she came to my shop."

"I see." Stephanie walked into the kitchen, a place as elegant and large as the parlor, but there was a breakfast nook by the back door that seemed much smaller and cozier. A coffee pot was already on the table there, and Stephanie grabbed a mug from the counter and motioned for

Casey to follow her.

A tall, thin woman, straight as a Martinet, walked into the kitchen, a frown on her face. Casey thought she had to be in her mid to late fifties, but she almost looked as if she had come from another era. Her hair was steel gray, and she kept it braided at her neck.

"Stephanie, do you need help with anything?" she asked.

Stephanie waved a hand in the air. "I'm fine. Thank you, Gail."

The woman remained.

"This is a private conversation," Stephanie added quietly.

"The baby is with the gentleman. If there's anything—"

"Gail. Enjoy yourself. Watch a program. Lie down, read a book," Stephanie said, smiling at the woman. "It's okay. You don't have to be busy every second. Trust me, you are appreciated."

The woman smiled, cast a suspicious glance at Casey, and then left at last.

When they were seated across from one another, Stephanie poured Casey some coffee and indicated that she should help herself to cream and sugar from the servers by the pot.

"So, did my sister owe you money?" Stephanie asked, sipping her coffee.

"No."

"Are you here to ask for some kind of money?"

"No," Casey said. She winced and stirred in the cream she'd just added to her cup.

"Did you even know my sister, or is this some kind of a prank...or worse?" Stephanie asked, staring at her hard.

"No, I swear it's not a prank." Casey winced inwardly again and then took a deep breath.

"Lena was worried," she said in a rush, trying to figure out how to tell Stephanie the truth. "She...she doesn't—didn't—believe Anthony just fell. And she was worried for herself. But more than that, she was afraid for the baby. And now, she's gone. But... I can't forget the things she said to me, and I felt I had to warn you. Tell you just how frightened she was and how worried she was. And that...well, it's inconceivable, but she believes even Annette could be in danger." She suddenly sat straighter. "The baby. Where is she?"

Stephanie smiled at that, yet it seemed she looked at Casey more warily. "Annette is fine. I'm always with her. I don't even leave her with the housekeeper. She's with a relative."

"Um..."

"A relative on *my* side of the family," Stephanie said. She was quiet for a few minutes.

Casey sipped her coffee, still feeling like a fool. She had said what needed to be said. Now, she had to get out—and hope she'd fulfilled the mission given to her by a ghost. She no longer wanted to be haunted.

Except...

It hadn't been that bad. She'd enjoyed talking to Lena.

Or to herself, if she'd made up the ghost in her head.

"You know, Lena wasn't born rich. We grew up in Gretna. My mother was a teacher, and my dad was an accountant. We didn't want for anything, but they were hardworking, and we grew up with that ethic. Oh! And Anthony—did you know him?"

"No, I'm sorry. I didn't."

"He was great." Stephanie paused to smile. "He was like a nerdy hippie, if that makes any sense. He would have done great things with the company. Part of the Marceau money is in prescription drugs. Anthony wanted to make sure prices went down. He wanted the company restaurants to donate food and supplies to food kitchens. He had plans...Lena meant to keep those plans, and I want to live up to their legacy, but I don't know how they battled that board of directors. They exhaust me. And I never wanted to be in business. I illustrate children's books. Or I *did*. I'm afraid money was never my high point—money or math."

"Miss Harrow, money means nothing next to life," Casey said. "I know that—"

"I'm the legal guardian. I was made Annette's legal guardian in the event that something happened to Anthony or Casey." Stephanie gripped her cup with both hands. "I can't leave this baby. I'm careful about what I do. I don't want the money. I don't know how well you knew my sister, and I don't know if you're a sham."

"A sham? I'm sorry—"

"Don't you run a voodoo or magic or ghost shop?" Stephanie asked. "I think I remember Lena saying something about your place. A Beautiful Mind. You're a medium, right? Well, I'm afraid I don't put much stock in crystal balls, Miss Nicholson."

"Stephanie, I'm not a medium. I don't even own a crystal ball. Oh, I have a cute little display with a beautiful gypsy holding one, but I don't—"

"Thank you for coming. I see you've finished your coffee. May I see you to the door?"

"Yes, yes. Thank you for seeing me. And please, I know your sister was afraid—"

"You think I don't know my sister didn't commit suicide?" Stephanie asked, angry. "But I can't go to the cops. Tell them that someone—without even touching her—forced her to take a bunch of pills. That, facing death, she defied a knife or a bullet, knowing it would at least prove she had been murdered. I can't even come up with an answer myself—"

"Annette. The baby..." Casey said.

"What?"

"She bargained. Lena convinced the killer it would be best to let her lock the baby in her childproof safe room and have her take the pills voluntarily—than have her fight and have defensive wounds, showing everyone that she had been murdered."

Stephanie gasped, and tears suddenly filled her eyes. But then she blinked them away and cleared her face of any emotion.

It was clear Stephanie didn't want to acknowledge that Casey might have had a little help coming up with the scenario. After all, she'd just said she didn't put much stock in things like that. The information possibly coming from her dead sister's ghost might be a bit much to take, especially right now. Casey didn't want to add to the woman's grief, so she didn't say any more.

"I'll...uh...see you out. Unless you think you can convince a homicide detective your words are true. Anyway...I...I need you to go now," Stephanie said.

"Of course. I'm so sorry," Casey whispered.

She stood. She didn't need to be shown to the door. She had done what she had been asked to do. There was nothing more.

She glanced at her watch. It was nearly ten. She drove to the shop, trying to shake the feeling that she wasn't done with it all yet as she drove. But when she got to A Beautiful Mind, Jared and Lauren were there. They had already opened and were speaking to a group of customers about one of their displays.

Casey found herself waving and retreating to her reading room. She kept her tarot cards there, and it was set up with a table and comfortable chairs.

And her computer. She began research on the Marceau company. She had been looking for just about an hour when Lauren came back, tapping on the door and opening it, looking concerned.

"Um, there's someone out here insisting they see you—" she began.

She didn't finish. A man came up behind her, shoving the door all the way open and turning to stare at Lauren.

"Thank you," he told her, not pushing her exactly, but urging her out.

Casey leapt to her feet, staring at him, frowning and angry. He was a very tall man, about six-foot-four, wearing a business suit—in New Orleans, in the French Quarter. He had dark hair cut short but a little longer across his forehead, and broad shoulders with a build to go with his height.

She didn't care. This was her shop.

"You don't have an appointment," she said icily. "And you have been rude to Lauren. I'll thank you to exit the store before I call the police," she informed him.

He wasn't daunted in the least. He leaned on her table and stared at her hard.

"What were you doing at the Marceau house? How are you involved? Who are you working for?"

"What?"

She sank back into her chair. To her horror, it was the wrong move. He walked around the table in two steps and stared at her computer.

"Right. You know nothing about what happened, and yet you're on the Marceau home page?"

"I—I—"

"I repeat, what were you doing at the Marceau house?" he demanded.

He was imposing. She was almost afraid. But to her surprise, her fighting spirit rose to the fore.

"Who the hell are you? And how dare you barge in here like this?" she managed.

She was a good eight inches shorter than him, but she squared her shoulders, set her hands on her hips, and stared him down.

"Did someone pay you?" he asked her.

"Pay me? For what?" she asked. He was accusing and questioning her. But about what? She was honest, they had good business practices. She couldn't begin to understand this man's problem.

She took a deep breath and said, "I don't know who you are. I don't know who you think I am. I suggest you tell me just what it is you want, and then perhaps kindly remove yourself from these premises."

"What do you have to do with Marceau Industries Incorporated? Why were you pretending to be friends with Lena Marceau?"

He had eyes that were such a curious hazel color, they seemed to burn as he stared at her. The sound of his voice was deep and harsh and determined. She could imagine him as a cop in an interrogation room, and she doubted many *didn't* shiver and garble out the truth when he looked at them like that and spoke as he did.

She sank into her chair.

"I don't have anything to do with the Marceau company," she said.

"What were you doing at the house? Did you even know Lena?"

She looked at him and said softly, "Yes. I knew Lena. She liked this shop."

He backed up a step, crossing his arms over his chest, still watching her like a hawk. "Are you friends with Justin Marceau? Related to or friends with or on the payroll of Barton Quincy, Larry Swenson, or Harry Miller?"

"Sadly, I'm not on anyone's payroll except my own," she snapped. "I don't know Barton Quincy, Larry Swenson, or Harry Miller."

"You were at the Marceau house."

"Yes."

"Why?"

"I should have gone before. I—I knew Lena, yes. And I know she never believed her husband just accidentally fell off a building. Or jumped. And she was afraid. And she was worried for Stephanie and Annette. I went because...I think it's important for Stephanie to know that Lena was worried."

"What took you so long to go see Stephanie then?"

She shook her head. "I—I didn't know Stephanie. Just Lena. I was afraid Stephanie would think I was crazy or after something. Look," she said, "I—I woke up this morning and decided it was early enough, that I could try to speak with Stephanie. She just needed to know that Lena was worried—had been worried. Afraid. I know nothing about the company. We make a decent living here. We have a huge mortgage on this place, but between us—my two partners and I—we get by. I don't know why in God's name you think someone would pay me to go to the Marceau house. No one did. You can ask Stephanie."

"I did."

"Well, then, you know what was said."

"Right. A quack from a shop combining every mystical thing in history came and started warning her to be careful."

"I'm not a quack."

"But you're supposed to be some kind of medium?"

"Argh!" She let out a cry of frustration. "I am not a medium. I read tarot cards. I read people. I sing in the street or in here sometimes with Jared. That's it. That's...that's it," she repeated.

She wasn't about to tell this man that Lena's ghost had visited her.

"So, who the hell are you? And what right do you have barging in here to question me and make fun of my place of business?" she demanded.

He leaned on the table; his face so close to hers.

"I'm Lena's cousin," he said softly.

He straightened and took a business card out of his jacket pocket, letting it fall onto the table.

"I'm Lena's cousin," he repeated, "Special Agent Ryder McKinley. Contact me when you feel you have more messages from beyond," he snapped.

Then he turned and left.

She heard the bell ring above the door, and then Jared and Lauren were in the room, staring at her worriedly.

* * * *

Ryder left the shop, trying to get a grip on his temper. He'd had no right to burst into the store and advance on the woman as he had, but before taking the baby and trying to keep her quiet to home in on Stephanie's conversation, he'd gotten a good look at her.

He'd wondered if she would go back to her shop and put on a ridiculously colored turban and a gypsy skirt and call herself Madam Something or Other.

But she hadn't. He'd followed her, of course. He'd watched her go in, and he'd waited, observing the store and its surroundings.

Then he'd gone in.

And had gotten nothing.

She knows something—or worse.

She's working for someone.

One of New Orleans' best coffee shops was up the road, so he headed that way, glancing at his watch.

William Marley would be removed from his resting place in an hour and a half. Adam had a friend at the office of the district attorney over in Mississippi, and the body or cremains—whatever remained at this point—

would be taken over the state line to be examined, and so those who had contact with him before, during, and after his death could be questioned.

Ryder knew it would serve no purpose for him to go to Mississippi. The tests would take time. It was unlikely there would be much soft tissue left, but whatever remained might well prove something.

And if not...

There was this woman. The interesting one. Intriguing.

She hadn't put on a turban. In fact, she had looked like a scholar studying her computer.

With the site for Marceau Industries Incorporated displayed.

He judged her age to be in the mid to late twenties—he didn't think she'd hit thirty yet. She was medium height with long, slim legs, brilliant blue eyes, and hair darker than his. A striking woman, and about Lena's age when she died. He had to admit, it was conceivable the two had been friends.

And still...

Why suddenly go to Stephanie with a warning?

He walked into the coffee shop, glad they brewed coffee so strong a spoon could almost stand up in the cup. But as he entered the queue for the outdoor seating, he noticed Justin Marceau sitting at a table with Barton Quincy.

The offices for Marceau Industries Incorporated were in the Central Business District.

It was curious that they were in the French Quarter.

They hadn't seen him yet, so he leaned against the counter, waiting for his order and trying to see if he could discern any of their conversation.

He only heard one line.

"Stephanie won't vote for it. She's following everything Lena wanted to a T."

It was Justin who spoke.

Barton replied in a hushed but passionate whisper that Ryder couldn't catch.

Ryder's coffee order came up.

He walked over to the table and greeted the men in a friendly fashion. "Hey, Justin. And it's Barton, right? Barton Quincy? We met at Lena and Anthony's wedding. Ryder McKinley," he reminded Barton.

"Oh. Oh," Barton Quincy said, frowning. "I thought you worked for the FBI or something. I saw you at the funeral, but I thought you were back in D.C. or wherever now. What brings you back to these parts?"

"Lena was my cousin, so Steph is my cousin, too. Obviously. I wanted to check up on her and make sure the baby is doing well," Ryder said easily. "I had a little time off. I just finished a case, and it seemed some R and R was in order."

He kept his tone light and friendly.

Justin seemed nervous. Barton tried to assure him that everything was going well.

"I hear you set up security in the house for Stephanie before you left," Barton said.

"He did," Justin said with enthusiasm. "Guards on the property twenty-four-seven. And cameras in every room."

"A little overkill, don't you think?" Barton looked up at Ryder, not a twitch in tone when he said the word *kill*.

Ryder grimaced. "Well, the girls and I—Lena and Steph—grew up close. We were friends, as well as family. It still bothers me I didn't realize Lena was that deeply depressed about Anthony's death. Of course, Stephanie is an aunt, not a mom, so she's a little paranoid about making sure nothing happens to Annette. The girl is a little whirlwind. This way, Steph can grab things from the kitchen and keep an eye on the baby up in the playroom." Ryder made a show of looking around. "You two are a little out of your neighborhood."

"I had some shopping to do on Royal Street," Barton said. "Thought we could meet here."

"You two don't go into the office every day?"

Barton laughed. "This fellow? Work?" he teased. "Justin's surname is Marceau, you know."

"Hey! I'm available whenever needed," Justin said. "I did a great job at the last marketing meeting."

Barton shrugged and glanced at his watch then rose. "Well, I've got to get back. It was nice seeing you again, um, Ryder. Are you going to be here long?"

"I'm not sure just how long yet," Ryder said pleasantly. "I never know when I'll get a call to be somewhere, so..."

He left off, grinning and shrugging.

"Anyway, I should be off, too," Ryder said. "Good to see you both. I'm glad to know that when I can't be here, Stephanie has great people to call on."

Justin lifted a hand in goodbye. Ryder went down the street and then slipped behind a colonnade in a building hallway.

He watched the two men as they rose and parted.

Justin started for Canal.

Barton Quincy paused, looking up and down the street. Ryder wasn't sure, but he thought the man was watching one shop. Just one shop.

"A Beautiful Mind."

Did he know Casey Nicholson? Was that why he was looking at the shop?

Or had he seen Casey head to the Marceau house? Was he—like Ryder—curious as to why the woman had gone to see Stephanie?

Curious, too, as to just what Casey Nicholson knew about the death of Lena Marceau.

* * * *

Casey left the shop that day as early as she could.

She had to forget Lena Marceau, Stephanie Harrow, and the angry FBI guy who had shown up in the store.

It was hot, and she was done early enough to head for the pool at her fourplex before the mosquitoes got too bad.

Her friends teased her that she lived at an old folks' home—retired people rented the other three apartments in the building.

She loved the three couples, though. They watched out for both her and the building.

Plus, they brought her baked goods all the time. Only Miss Lilly—who had been an Olympic swimmer in her day—spent much time in the pool, and that was early. Miss Lilly might be found in the water any time after 6:00 A.M. Her husband, Joe, would sit in one of the lawn chairs and watch her, waving a hand and smiling and pretending he didn't hear her any time she suggested he get in—he needed exercise.

But at this time of night, the place was hers.

And the water felt good. So good. The temperature had been in the eighties and nineties all day, and many people might have thought the water in the pool was a bit too hot—like a lukewarm bath.

It didn't bother Casey at all. She loved the heat. And there was something special about water. She swam a bit, then just floated on her back and watched as the sun disappeared, and night slowly came on.

She wondered if she should go back to the cemetery and see if Lena was there. Did ghosts hang out in graveyards when they weren't busy haunting people, asking them to take care of something for them? She had first seen Lena's ghost in the cemetery.

And she'd fainted. Like a true coward.

She was a chicken. She simply hadn't believed in ghosts.

But would she rather a ghost haunt her, or accept the possibility that she was totally losing her mind?

She wasn't sure which she'd prefer at that point. She just knew that the water felt good. She tried to turn her mind to life and her commitments. She had promised that she would give a NOLA history and cemetery speech in the shop in two days for Miss Lilly's granddaughter's small study group. She needed to brush up on a few facts.

She had managed to think about the city and its history and enjoy the feeling of just floating in the water, looking up at the darkening sky, when she heard a hushed whisper. She blinked.

Lena was back. And she seemed to be drifting in the sky.

"Get out. Get out of the pool as quickly as you can!"

"What?"

"There's someone here—someone's out there. And he's...he's dressed in black. He's stalking you. He's in the bushes in the back of the neighbor's yard, watching you. Get in and lock your door and don't come out!" Lena's ghost warned.

Whether she was crazy or not, Casey jumped out of the pool. She grabbed her towel off the lounger and raced for the back door to the fourplex, once a shotgun house with a hall that ran from the front to the back and offered doors to the four apartments.

She threw open the door and slammed into someone. She nearly screamed.

Someone tall and dark and ridiculously solid, yet still nothing but a hulking shape in the night.

But then the shape spoke.

"Miss Nicholson. I'm sorry if I startled you. A woman who said her name was Lilly let me in and said that I'd find you out back," he said.

Him!

The man from the shop.

"Oh, my God. What are *you* doing following me here? Coming to my home?" she demanded in a desperate whisper.

She only realized then that he was holding her, steadying her.

"Trying to make sure you don't get killed," he said, his tone dry...

And carrying a frightening ring of truth.

Chapter 4

Denial. Seriously. She couldn't really have spent the evening before chatting with a ghost. And if so, she had done what the ghost wanted.

She couldn't be in danger herself.

Casey shook her head, trying to make something that resembled sense and logic out of it all.

"Back up," she said. "I don't understand. There's no reason for anyone to want to kill me, to follow me," she said, speaking quickly, trying to regain her sense of balance.

She stepped back at last, realizing he'd still been holding her. She murmured, "I'm sorry. I'm sorry. I'm soaked, and I just got you all wet. But—wait! You're the one following me, you...how are you here? I don't...I don't owe you an apology. I..."

He couldn't have been whoever Lily had said was out back in the bushes. He was standing here.

He took her by the shoulders, calming her, and he met her eyes with his own as he spoke in a soft voice. "Why are you in such a panic? This isn't because I was at your back door just walking out. You were terrified of something else, Casey. What happened? What's going on?" He gently tightened his grip. "And why are you still shaking?"

"I'm not. I—"

She broke off. What did she say to an FBI agent who had already knocked her for being a so-called medium?

"There was a noise in the bushes. I guess it scared me. I—I thought someone was back there."

He froze and dropped his hands. A seriousness took over his entire demeanor. "Get in your room and lock the door after you lock this one and the front entry. When I'm back, I'll ring."

She nodded.

"I mean it, Casey. Do it. You may be in danger."

"Yes."

He stepped out the back. She watched him as he raced around the pool and disappeared into the hedges.

Lock the front door.

She hurried to do it and then slipped through her own door and locked it as well. For a moment, she stood there panting. Then she wasn't sure what to do.

"Lena?" she called.

But the ghost didn't answer.

She leaned against the door, holding tightly to her towel. She listened, but all she heard were the sounds of night—a car passing, a motorcycle, her neighbor's too-loud TV. But that was okay, Joe was hard of hearing and noise had never bothered her.

Then the buzzer to her apartment rang. She hit the button. "Yes?"

"Come let me in, if you will. Please."

"Okay."

She hurried to the front and opened the door. The agent was brushing leaves off his jacket.

"May I come in?" He took a deep breath. "Look, I apologize. I was an ass today. I was telling you the truth, though. Yes, I'm an agent, and yes, Lena was my cousin. And—"

"Yes, you were an ass today."

"I just said that." His lips tipped up in a small grin. "But everything I'm saying is true, and you know it. Lena was my second cousin, and I cared about her, deeply. And I care about Stephanie and the baby. Even if they had been strangers, what's going on here is cruel and heinous and could keep happening to innocent people." His eyes became more earnest than she thought possible. "I'm sorry I behaved badly. But this is serious. May we please talk?"

"I—yes. I just..."

She looked down at herself. She was still wearing her skimpy bikini with nothing more than the towel draped around her shoulders.

He glanced down briefly and then his eyes came right back to hers and stayed there. "I can wait while you change."

She nodded and turned down the hall, opening the door to her apartment.

He followed her in.

"Um...there's just one bedroom, up the stairs," she told him. *Why?* "The kitchen, dining, and parlor are all right here, as you can see. Help yourself to anything. I'll be right down."

Upstairs, she shed her suit and rinsed off quickly then grabbed clothing—a pair of jeans and a tee shirt—and hurried back downstairs, towel-drying her hair as she did.

He was seated at the dining room table, looking at his phone.

He hadn't helped himself to anything.

"Um—coffee?" she asked, a bit flustered. "And did you find anything? I mean, you tried to find out if someone was outside, right?"

"They're gone."

She sat across from him, studying his features. She hadn't realized before that he was so attractive. He'd barged in like a large ape, and that hadn't called for much of a fair assessment. He had a great jawline. And he was, she had to admit...compelling. His look was rough and rugged, yet almost classical with the clean line of his nose, the set of his eyes, and his cheekbones.

And, of course, I'm sitting here like a drowned rat.

Did that matter? He thought she was in danger. Lena had been murdered. But as far as she knew, no one else knew that Lena had told her anything.

Why would she be in danger?

"I am sincerely sorry for being so angry today," he said again, his tone low and modulated, and she thought sincere.

"Okay," she said slowly.

"You really knew Lena?"

"Yes. I really knew her. Not well, but she did talk to me a few times before... She came into the shop quite a bit."

"Have you seen her recently?" he asked.

"She's dead," Casey said.

"I know." He paused and softened his voice. "So, have you seen her recently?"

"What?" she asked sharply. "Look, you have the wrong idea, but I'm sure that's my fault. I majored in psychology, but I didn't care for the work I was offered after I got out of college. My friends were having the same problem. But I never, ever say I'm a medium, if that's what you're getting at. I have a dozen books on reading tarot cards, and I like them because you can lead them to say what you want. I swear to you, I try to make people happier about themselves, and that is it. I don't—I don't summon ghosts. I don't run seances. But it's true, I also read tea leaves. I have a dozen books on that, too—"

"And dozens of psychology books, I see," he said.

Just outside what would be the partition between the dining room and parlor if one existed, were her bookshelves. They lined both walls.

"I love the human mind. Strangest thing is it's the hardest thing in the world to fathom when you're working on your own."

He nodded for a minute, studying her, his eyes enigmatic.

"Lena Marceau did not kill herself. You are right in that."

"Um...are *you* a medium?" she asked him. "Has she...come to you?"

"Are you mocking me?" he asked her.

"I wouldn't dream of mocking a federal agent," she said sweetly.

He was quiet, studying her for a minute, and then he said, "I don't know why she hasn't come to me."

"Pardon?"

He slid his elbows on the table and leaned closer to her. "I don't know why she hasn't come to me. And I have had your background checked. Graduated with honors, worked a few places, bought the shop on St. Anne. You don't even have a parking ticket. Now, that's not easy, living here. Your parents are Gerome and Marie, who moved to Arizona when your dad's doctor suggested he needed a drier climate. You were born here, and you've been here since, other than for a six-month European study session during your junior year. You seem to be aboveboard in every way. Then again, that's just the type of person certain criminal elements try to rope in. So..."

"Um—so?"

"Either you have been paid to cause trouble—I doubt that after tonight—you just want something from Stephanie Marceau, or my cousin came to you."

"Look, I knew Lena—"

"And she's still talking to you."

He said it flatly, staring at her hard. She felt a sizzle race through her, and she didn't know if it was a touch of ice or a bit of fire.

"Are you trying to have me committed?" she asked.

"No. Look, I am an FBI agent, but I'm part of a special division called the Krewe of Hunters. We investigate...unusual cases. I'm not a medium. Mediums claim to have the ability to summon and talk to certain spirits—and maybe they can in some instances. But in my experiences with the dead—and they have been extensive—not all stay around to be summoned. Many who remain do so because they worry about the future of their descendants. They feel they need to guard a certain place or even see to it that history is remembered. Or because life was stolen from them in one way or another, and they have to see justice is done and ensure other lives aren't taken."

She stared back at him.

Could this be legitimate? Or was he trying to see that she was committed to an institution? Could they do that to her just because she believed she had seen a ghost?

They'd have to lock up half of New Orleans.

"Please," he said quietly.

She winced. "You don't have any recording devices on you, do you?"

He shook his head. "No. I swear."

She took a deep breath and decided to trust him with the truth. "I saw her first in the cemetery. It freaked me out so badly, I passed out twice and landed in the hospital for the night. They thought I had heatstroke. I thought maybe I did, too, seeing a dead woman. Then she came to the shop when I was alone last night. We talked for a long time." She focused her eyes on his. "Yes, she was murdered."

"Why haven't I seen her yet?" It was an introspective question, and he seemed hurt. But he gave himself a shake—both mentally and physically, Casey thought. "So, how? That's the question I keep getting when I try to pursue this case. But it may get better."

Casey shook her head. "May get better?"

"We had cremains disinterred today. I don't think even Anthony was this killer's first victim. A man who was on the board may have been—an old and dear friend to Elijah. He had no heart condition and mysteriously died of a heart attack. Luckily, over the state line."

"Luckily?"

"For me, not for him. I'm sorry. For the Krewe. It's a good thing. We can step in if anything is proven."

"You dug someone up today?"

"This is New Orleans. We didn't dig."

She shook her head. "No, no. I mean—"

"Yes, we exhumed a body. Please, tell me what Lena has told you."

Casey let out a breath. "We talked a lot," she said softly. "I don't know if you noticed those chairs by the coffee and tea stand, but...she just showed up there and sat in a chair. And she begged me not to pass out again, and I didn't. I knew someone would think I was crazy if I went to Stephanie with Lena's warning, but she was so desperate for someone's help..."

"You're not crazy," he told her.

She stood suddenly. "Special Agent McKinley, she was here tonight. She warned me to get out of the pool, said that someone was watching me. That they were in black and...I wonder if she went off, trying to find the person, too." She hesitated, wincing again as she looked at him. "Do ghosts have...rules? Or I should say, they can't just get anywhere by twitching their noses or anything. Can they?"

He shook his head and studied her again. "My special unit of the FBI is comprised of people who are part of the less than one percent of the population who has the sixth sense, or whatever it is. And recognize what they have. There are degrees to everything. Some people get a chill. Some see or hear things in their dreams, which is really nice. For instance, a mom comes to her children in a dream and assures them she's fine, that she's back with their dad. That kind of thing. Others..." He paused and shrugged. "Ghosts have to learn how to get around. They're like children, discovering more every day. But from all my experiences and those that have been shared with me by my colleagues, they can't be in more than one place at a time. And have you heard that saying? 'Beware of hitch-hiking ghosts?' Well, yes, ghosts like to hitch-hike or slide onto airplanes. I have a friend whose brother died in an accident, and he loves nothing more than to find flights where first class hasn't been fully booked. He pretends he's kicking back and enjoying the champagne."

"He can't drink champagne," Casey murmured.

He smiled. "Lena was here. Tonight."

"As I said, she warned me to get out of the pool and lock myself in."

He shook his head. "She wasn't out there. I hopped a couple of fences and looked around the general area. Whoever it was is gone. And so is Lena," he said. "All right, did she explain to you what happened by any chance? I mean, she took pills. Why? Did someone force her? Who?"

"A man in black."

"A man in black?"

"She couldn't see his identity. He wore black. Pants, shirt, mask—one that covered his entire face except his eyes. But she was convinced her killer was male."

"How?" The word was almost a whisper.

"She bargained. She told the killer she'd fight him tooth and nail, and the world would know she'd been murdered if he didn't let her put the baby in the safe room and lock her in. I guess the killer figured he had time to see that the baby had an accident somewhere along the line. So, Lena took care of the baby, leaving her where only Stephanie could get to her, and she took the pills." She frowned then. "I wonder what stopped her from fighting back once the baby was safe."

"Torture, maybe."

"Pardon?"

"Maybe she was afraid if she reneged on the agreement, the killer would torture her until she couldn't bear it and gave up the baby again."

"But once she was dead—"

"The killer couldn't get to Annette. The lock on the door is computer-driven—you must have the code to get into the room. Only Lena and Stephanie have the code. And Lena could leave the baby in there because it's completely childproof. Annette's mattress is on the floor, the outlets have child plugs, there is no other furniture, just a plastic play desk and tons of toys. Annette could have cried herself to sleep alone in there until Stephanie arrived—that's the worst that could have happened."

"Oh," Casey murmured. Then she shook her head. "That's what I know. And..."

"And?"

"I think she might have saved me tonight. But I still don't understand. Why would someone come after me? Unless the man skulking around my neighbor's yard is just your run-of-the-mill peeping Tom, creep, or burglar."

He hesitated again.

"Oh, please. Come on. I don't know you, and you just convinced me to tell you I had a long conversation with a ghost. You came here. You came to me. You accused me of all kinds of things, and everything you know about me is boringly true. Have the decency to tell me what is going on," Casey said. She hadn't realized she was so angry until she stood, slamming her palms down on the table and speaking to him with her face just inches from his.

"Sorry," she said, moving back.

But he was smiling. "Good. You need to be fierce. You know what's going on. My cousin was murdered. And you know more about it than I do."

"Yes, but—"

"I knew Lena wouldn't kill herself. But forensically and by law, there was absolutely no way to prove it. She took the pills, and there was no sign the house had been broken into, or she had been forced in any way. She succeeded in her objective—she saved her baby. But I do believe whoever is behind this intends to kill Stephanie and the baby *and* anyone who gets in their way. I'm not sure what they're afraid of. They must realize you'd be a laughingstock if you went to the papers or the police and told people that Lena came to you and told you what had happened. But now that we know, we look for a way to prove it. I was frustrated, but I work with great people. We found out about the death of William Marley. And the man who founded our unit happens to be in the right circles in politics no matter who is at the helm. He managed to get us an exhumation order. Besides that, I believed from the get-go that Lena's killer—and William's and Anthony's—had to be someone in the corporation. Someone not happy with the way it's being run, or who wants to take over completely. There's only one family member left on the board. Justin Marceau. But he has his title, and he takes part in their marketing and promotion. Right now, they're heavily invested in the pharmaceutical drug trade. Elijah, Anthony, and Lena weren't as concerned with profits as they were with the wonders the right drugs could do for people—curing illnesses and prolonging life. So, there's Justin for one. And then there's the rest of the board. Barton Quincy, Harry Miller, and Larry Swenson. Barton has seniority, and he's the director of operations. Larry Swenson is his assistant—basically up after Barton—and Harry Miller's title is sales director."

"How did they get into the house? I saw cameras—"

"Amazingly, there was a blackout in the footage around the time Lena was killed. And according to the board, they were all together at the offices in the CBD when Lena died. Except for Justin, who came over early to warn Lena about what the board planned to discuss at the meeting. And he and Gail Reeves, the housekeeper, ran into each other at the bookstore in the Garden District. Justin gave her a ride back to the house. It was her afternoon off."

"Is Gail still there now, with Stephanie and the baby?"

He nodded. "Don't worry. Her alibi was airtight. Her book club had a meeting. Three people let me know she was there the entire time. One problem, of course, is Justin. I don't know if he's outright guilty or guilty of collaboration. Or if he's in danger." He shrugged. "I have a full-time security guard at the house. I hired a few retired agents. I know three of them, and they're on duty twenty-four-seven."

"Good," Casey murmured. "But back to me—"

"I saw Barton Quincy staring at your shop today. He and Justin were together at the coffee shop by your place. It seemed a distance to go for coffee from the CBD. Barton said something about needing something in the French Quarter."

"Well, that is feasible."

"It is." He scrubbed a hand down his face. "I'm sorry. I do believe everything you've told me. I had to be...sure. You'd be surprised by the number of naïve people who need money and get suckered by criminals. And while you might have had a run-of-the-mill peeping Tom back there, burglar or whatever—you may be in danger."

They were both quiet for a minute.

"Aren't you going to tell me you can take care of yourself?" he asked her.

Casey laughed softly. "No. I'm good at a lot of things. My best defense against anything bad is screaming like a banshee. I've never taken Kung Fu, and I've never been to a shooting range. I don't even like carving up meat."

He smiled at that. "Okay. Good."

"That's good?"

"Yep. You won't give me a hard time when I want you protected."

"And what is your plan here?" she asked.

"I'm not sure yet," he told her.

"Okay."

They sat in silence for another few minutes. He was thinking—obviously. But she was beginning to feel a bit awkward.

"Uh, would you like some coffee?" she asked.

A slow smile crept onto his lips. When he wanted to be, he could be nice. And that slow smile of his was almost...charming.

Maybe *charming* wasn't the word.

Seductive.

"You would like coffee, right?"

"Dinner," he said.

"Oh, well, I'm not sure what I have—" She tucked a stray strand of hair behind her ear and licked her lips. His eyes followed the movement, and she could have sworn she saw his eyes darken.

"This is New Orleans. Restaurants abound. Let's go to dinner."

"Dinner. Oh. Okay. It's getting a bit late—"

"This is New Orleans," he repeated.

"Are you asking me out to dinner?" she asked.

"I am." He winked.

"I'm not dressed—"

"I do believe you're one of those people who could wear a potato sack and still look fine," he said lightly. "We won't go anywhere fancy. Just out. There's a place off Magazine Street—"

"Hmm, people sometimes dress up on Magazine Street."

"I said *off* Magazine," he told her. "Family place. The owners are friends. He's first-generation Italian, and her family is Creole. Great, casual food."

"You sold me," Casey said.

"Make sure to lock up."

She locked her door, and as they were leaving through the main entrance, Miss Lilly came out of her apartment, smiling as she saw them.

"I see you found Casey okay, Ryder," she said.

"I did. Thank you for sending me through, Miss Lilly. As much as I appreciate your help, please don't let anyone else in. There have been some break-ins in the neighborhood."

"Oh, my! Well, thank you for telling me. I'll make sure the place is locked. And I'll tell the others. My, my, what a pretty couple you two make! Good to see you going out, Casey." She looked at Ryder. "This girl just spends too much time working. Not that I don't love the shop. I do. Anyway, you two go on out on your date. I'll see we all know we need to keep the main doors locked up good and tight."

"Oh, Miss Lilly, we're not—" Casey began. But she *was* going out on a date...

"We're really just friends, Miss Lilly," she corrected.

They weren't even friends.

Miss Lilly waved a hand in the air. "Get on out so I can lock up and get back to my program."

"Will do. A pleasure," Ryder told her.

They walked down the path to the street. Casey automatically started toward her little hybrid car, but Ryder said, "Mind if I drive? I know where I'm going."

"Ah, fine."

He opened the passenger door for her, and she slid in. Her arm grazed his as she did, and she felt a current of sensation rush through her, nearly causing goose bumps. He walked around to the driver's seat and was quiet as he pulled out onto the street.

"So, hmm. How long have you been an FBI agent?" Casey asked him.

"Four years. Before that, I was a detective in Baltimore."

"Baltimore? I got the impression you were from Louisiana."

"I am. But I went to college up there and stayed and became a cop. And then a detective. And then I went to the academy and right into the Krewe." He was watching the road, but he shrugged and looked at her quickly. "I saw my first ghost when my grandfather died. We were close. My dad was a cop, and one day, my grandfather's ghost warned him that one of their supposed snitches was in on the hard stuff himself. Since my dad was suspicious, the snitch arranged for an accident. Because he knew, my dad avoided the shootout intended for him in an alley. The problem when I worked as a detective in Baltimore is a lot like the problem we have here. You can't go to court, claiming a ghost told you what happened."

"No, I read somewhere that they ruled out spectral evidence after the witch trials in the Massachusetts Bay Colony," Casey said.

"And it's a good thing. People can make up anything."

"But you don't think I'm making anything up."

He glanced her way again.

"I know you're not."

They'd reached the restaurant.

It was off the main street, rustic and charming with picnic tables outside and nicely manicured foliage. Casey couldn't believe there was a restaurant she hadn't been to in the city, but New Orleans was filled with quaint little neighborhoods within neighborhoods, and she believed the restaurant catered to locals rather than tourists.

A middle-aged woman met them at the hostess stand and greeted Ryder warmly, clearly delighted to see him. She seemed happy to meet Casey, as well.

"So, you finally bring a beautiful girl to my restaurant," the woman said. "I'm Felice Barone—Felice Beauchamp Barone since we are Creole and Italian. The best of both, I believe! My husband and I, we are the owners. Owners and operators, cooks, busboys, and bottle washers," she said cheerfully. "I am delighted to meet you," she told Casey. She grew serious, looking at Ryder. "I thought you went back north. Back to work after...I am still so sorry, *cher.*"

"I did, but I'm back to give Stephanie a hand," Ryder said. "And, of course, if I am trying to impress a friend, I bring her here."

They chatted for a few more minutes and were then seated at an inside table. Casey hadn't cared where they sat when offered inside or outside seating. Then again, Ryder hadn't asked her. He had pointed to the table he wanted, causing Felice Barone to laugh. "This one, he thinks he's Italian. The old mob men, they had to make sure they were facing the door. You never have your back to the door."

"She's right. I like my back to the wall," Ryder said.

"An FBI thing?" Casey asked him.

"No." He chuckled. "I think I saw *The Godfather* at an impressionable age. But yeah, just a smart thing when you never know who you may run into—or who may be looking for you."

Felice had given them a corner square table so both could have their backs to the wall and then left them, assuring them that their waitress was one of her best.

"You can't honestly believe anyone is after me in an off-the-beaten-path restaurant, do you?" Casey asked when Felice was gone.

"No. If you go through that kind of trouble to make a murder look like suicide, you probably wouldn't ruin it by publicly attacking someone."

"Good. It will be great to eat without...watching the door," Casey said.

Their waitress arrived. She was pleasant and knew Ryder and greeted him warmly. She gave them the list of specials, suggesting that one have a Creole dish, and the other an Italian specialty so they could split them.

Ryder looked politely at Casey.

"I don't care what I eat," she said. "I mean, I'm sure it's going to be wonderful, whatever it is."

"Crawfish etouffee—it's the best here. And..."

"Lasagna!" Casey said.

"You're fond of Italian food?" Ryder asked her.

"I watched a lot of *Garfield* cartoons."

"Pardon?"

"*Garfield*! The cat, from Jim Davis."

"Oh, right. The fat cat that loves lasagna."

"You watch *Garfield*?" She smiled.

"Two-year-old little cousin," he reminded her with a grin.

"Ah."

The food came quickly, and it was wonderful. They both tried to be polite and wound up trying to put helpings of each dish on each other's plates at the same time, touching, apologizing, and then spilling food. But they finally got it together.

Casey was especially enjoying the crawfish etouffee when she looked up.

Someone was coming in the front door—someone who slipped in as a man was exiting.

Someone who wasn't alive.

"Ryder, I see her. She's just coming in. Do you see her?" Casey whispered.

He did. He almost stood, but apparently controlled himself quickly enough. He watched as Lena came up, gave Casey a quick smile, and leaned across the table to envelop Ryder in her arms.

Then she sat across from him.

Chapter 5

Ryder felt a wave of emotion rush through him. He'd wanted to see Lena, even in death—her spirit rather than the angelic and still form of her body. He initially hadn't thought her spirit had remained.

And mature adult or not, he'd not been able to fight the feeling of hurt and anger that had swept through him when he realized that her spirit *had* remained, but she'd chosen to go to someone else.

She had known he saw the dead. She'd been the one to help him *not* feel crazy when they were kids. She hadn't seen what he had, but she'd sensed things. And she had believed in him.

Now, she looked at him across the table.

"First, Casey, thank you," Lena said. "Ryder, I'm sorry."

"Why didn't you come to me?" Ryder whispered. "I was there in the house...right after. I was at the autopsy. The funeral. I stayed..."

"Ryder, I'm sorry," Lena said again. "But...well, frankly, it's not easy becoming a ghost. Maybe we don't want to accept it. Perhaps we just don't want to believe we're dead. Or maybe it's like a new birth, and we need to figure out how to exist in the world. It took me a while to...to understand that I could move and try to speak with people. At first...it was like sleep—a deep, deep sleep. Then I was in the cemetery and so afraid and alone...and, well, I finally made a few friends. Um, dead ones. And they helped me. By then...you were gone. And then I saw Casey. I'd met her at her store, and I knew she was kind and honest and...I'm afraid I sent her to the hospital from fright. But then I tried again, and I heard you were back, Ryder."

"I'm here, and we're working hard on this," Ryder assured her. "Casey has filled me in. Lena, I won't let it go. I will not let anything happen to Stephanie or Annette, I promise. But can you tell me anything about your attacker at all? Casey said you're sure it was a man. Do you know how he got in?"

"I have no idea. I keep the door locked. Gail keeps the door locked. Ryder, I was so scared, but not for myself. If anything had happened to Annette..."

As she broke off, he noted Casey was furtively looking around, possibly wondering how Ryder was conversing so easily without worrying about looking at Lena.

Experience. He toyed with his food and glanced her way now and then.

He knew she likely realized it looked as if he were just talking to Casey.

"I will not let anything happen to Annette," Ryder said firmly. "I swear it—on my life."

Lena smiled at him. "I believe you. You're my Superman, cousin. 'Truth, justice, and the American way,'" she quoted. "And I know you, Ryder. You'd be in this if it had been me or someone else—it's what you do. And I'm grateful for you."

"Well, let's see where we get," he said. "I need help from you. I need to find whoever did this to you."

"And Anthony," Lena added bitterly. "I never believed he just stretched too far to look at something and fell off a twenty-story building. And he definitely wasn't the type to commit suicide. But then again, neither was I—though we know what happened there. Ryder, you're my only hope," she said softly. "I mean," she added quickly, looking at Casey, "Casey, you were wonderful. I know you went to Stephanie. You must have since Ryder is here with you. And I've tried. I love my sister so much. I think she might have sensed something when I tried to speak with her, but she just doesn't...she doesn't see...the dead."

Ryder almost forgot himself, reaching out across the table to touch Lena's hand. But he winced and then drummed his fingers and glanced Casey's way again. She gave him a forced smile as if she were learning the art of conversing with the dead in public.

"Stephanie has put her trust in me. She's still at such a loss. You were her only sister."

"Maybe you can convince her I'm...okay. I mean, I'm here, but I will be able to find peace. They've been telling me—my dead friends—there comes a time when we all go, and there is goodness and something after.

A light. They claim they've seen loved ones come for other loved ones. I mean, I haven't, but...I'll be with Anthony. I must be able to tell him Annette is going to be fine. Ryder... How could anyone want money so much they'd kill like this? Elijah would never have handed control of the company to Anthony if he'd known it was a curse. Elijah was a good man, such a dear man. He believed in business, but he was also fair. And he made things people desperately needed easily available to them. But...is that it, Ryder? This was all over money?"

"Money and power," Ryder said. "Or so I believe. But I need to know more. And I think we're dealing with someone who is a true psychopath. Someone organized, capable of appearing perfectly normal—even in relationships—but lacking any true feelings or emotion."

"Someone who could kill without blinking and make sure they did it right," Lena said dryly.

"And it had to be someone close to you, the house, the family, or the corporation. That's why I need your help. And any little detail will help."

Lena glanced at Casey before answering and said softly, "I'm sorry. I'm sorry I dragged you into this. I'm just so frightened now for my sister and my baby."

"I'm all right," Casey said. And, looking at her, Ryder thought she was. Yes, she had been panicked and in denial. That might indicate that she was a normal person. How else did one react to suddenly realizing there was, in an already strange world, another world around her?

And she might be in casual clothing, but he hadn't lied to her. She was a beautiful, young woman, her best feature being her eyes. Their color was so blue it hinged on violet, and the depths of them always seemed to speak volumes.

Admittedly, he'd first thought her a quack, using her looks to help lure those who might believe she had a *friend line* to the beyond.

And now...

"Seriously," Casey added softly. "I want to help."

Lena smiled and said, "Thank you," softly to Casey and then turned back to Ryder. "I think he was about six feet tall. And I believe he was wearing contact lenses, making sure I couldn't recognize him if things went south. I don't know. He was in black—sweats, I believe. All-encompassing black. His hood covered his hair. I think he even had a voice box. It was all raspy as if it were coming through something. And he had wires around his face and neck under the sweatsuit top. I could still see them. I don't know how he got in. Gail was out—it was her afternoon off. Stephanie was coming over, but not for an hour or so. All I could do was bargain."

"You saved Annette's life," Ryder assured her.

They all fell silent. Felice came back to their table, pointing at their dishes.

"What's the matter? Suddenly you don't like the food?" she asked.

"Oh, no, the food is delicious," Casey assured her.

"Delicious as always," Ryder said.

Felice was frowning. "I don't know why you like this table. It's cold here! There must be something wrong with the air-conditioner. We must get that fixed. Would you like to move?"

"No, this is my table, and I love it, Felice," Ryder said. "You know that."

Felice smiled suddenly. "Look at the two of you. So close and...*whispery*. I guess you don't feel the cold. Ah, young love. You two can cuddle for warmth."

She left, and Lena laughed.

"You two do make an adorable couple."

"We're not a couple," Ryder and Casey said in unison.

"Well, okay, but you're both beautiful people, so...you would make a beautiful couple. Hey, trust me. Don't mess around. Life is short. I learned that saying to be the absolute truth."

"Oh, Lena," Ryder murmured.

Lena frowned and spoke in a panic. "I'm going to fade!"

"What?" Casey asked. "Fade?"

Lena shook her head. "It takes...well, learning. I'm learning to be a good ghost with a lot of help. But still...thank you both. We'll talk tomorrow. Oh! Ryder, you have Annette and Stephanie. And now, you can't let anything happen to Casey."

The last was barely a whisper. Casey's name sounded almost like a soft hiss.

Suddenly, Lena was gone.

Casey stared at Ryder. "Ghosts fade?"

"I can explain what I think I know," he told her. "I know many spirits, but...I've never been a ghost, and it seems the experience can be different from...ghost to ghost. From what I understand, it's not easy for them at first to...materialize, I guess. She'll need to rest, to gain strength again. Old ghosts can stay for longer periods of time. Some can even push buttons and sometimes move things. It's like anything—we learn to crawl, walk, and then run."

"You're so easy with all of this," she whispered.

"You think it's hard as an adult? Try being a kid telling someone their grandfather had given him warnings when that grandfather had been dead and interred for two years." He shrugged and smiled at her. "It takes time," he said softly.

"You mean...I may see other ghosts now?"

"When they choose to be seen."

"Oh." She groaned.

"It gets better. For tonight, I guess we should finish dinner. Then I'll get you back home."

"Take your time. I have a feeling I'll be up all night."

She would be up all night—listening. Afraid.

Ryder noticed the tension creeping into her face and body. "Maybe you shouldn't stay at your place."

"I could go to Lauren's house," she mused. Then she shook her head vehemently. "No. She lives with her grandmother, and I wouldn't put either of them in danger. Even though I'm not sure I'm in danger, I'm not brave enough to find out. I will lock all the doors, I'll—"

"No. We'll go by your place, you can get a few things, and we'll go to the Marceau house."

"What?"

It seemed the logical answer, especially since Ryder had no other solution. And while he doubted that Lena's killer would break into a house and risk capture, he'd somehow gotten into the Marceau house before.

"Look," Ryder said earnestly, "I promised to look after Stephanie and Annette. But now I'm worried about you, too. And you have the common sense to accept the fact you *might* be in danger. So, if we are all in one place, it will be much easier on me."

She seemed to weigh her options. "I still need to go to work in the morning."

"I'll get you there. But you can't be alone. And tomorrow, I'll get some help."

"You have friends with the NOPD?"

"I do. But I'm not calling them."

"Then—?"

He grinned and shrugged. "I have people."

She frowned at that, curious—and seemingly unconvinced. "I can't just go and stay at the Marceau house. I mean, I'm not invited—"

"You're invited. I'm inviting you."

"I don't think Stephanie liked me."

"Stephanie is still hurt. She's grieving, and you freaked her out. She'll want you there. She can't know the truth the way we do, doesn't quite understand, but she always knew that..."

"That?"

"Sometimes, it runs in families. We had a mutual great-grandparent who... Well, if it is something in the DNA, she was the one who passed it down. Stephanie knows there are people who *sense* things. She knows that I do. I didn't know much about you when I left the Marceau house after you did—"

"You were the relative—her side of the family—watching the baby when I was there."

"I was."

"I can't—"

"You must."

She sat back, shaking her head and biting her lip. Then she bowed her head slightly.

"Please," he said.

Her head still lowered, she nodded. She looked up and noted, "You still have crawfish on your plate."

"I'll take care of that," he told her. "You're leaving lasagna," he added.

"I'll take care of that," she said.

He smiled, and they finished their food.

He paid the tab, and they both assured Felice that the food had been beyond wonderful. And that they'd be back. He was afraid during the drive, and even as he waited for Casey to pack up a few things, that she would protest again.

But she didn't. She was silent during the trip to the Marceau house, and he didn't try to make idle conversation. At the mansion, he used the remote to open the gates and parked in the drive at the side of the house.

Stephanie was on the steps, chatting with Arnold Benson, one of the old friends Ryder had hired to watch the house. Little two-year-old Annette was in her arms. Stephanie was frowning, but the baby called out, "Hi!" and stretched out her arms.

"I'll explain," Ryder said briefly as he took Casey's small case and walked to the door. He was ready to take Annette from Stephanie, certain that she was reaching for him.

She wasn't.

Her outstretched arms were for Casey.

"Um, sorry. Hi. May I?" Casey asked Stephanie.

Stephanie didn't answer. She let Annette go.

The child was truly adorable. Like her mother had been, she was blonde. Little ringlets of a sunshine color framed her face. Her eyes were powder blue. Annette was, however, a typical two-year-old, wanting what she wanted.

"She knows you. She likes you," Stephanie said.

"Lena had her in the shop a few times. I set her up with a little tea set, and we played This Little Piggy Went to Market and a few other games," Casey explained. She held the baby and smiled as Annette giggled, said something in her baby language, and then showed Casey her nose.

Arnold Benson cleared his throat. Ryder quickly apologized and introduced him.

"An old friend. Arnold Benson was with the field office here for years. Arnie, Casey, Casey, Arnie."

Arnie smiled at Casey. Casey smiled back. Ryder figured she approved of his choice for a guard.

Arnie had shaved his head and looked as if he were retired from the World Wrestling Federation rather than the FBI.

"Nice to meet you," Casey said.

"Pleasure. So, is this lovely lady what really brought you back to NOLA?" Arnie asked Ryder.

"Casey is a friend. And I've been honest with you, Arnie. You know what brought me back."

"Yeah," Arnie said softly, glancing at Stephanie. "I just came out to do a grounds check. I have a little nook in the library where I can see more than a satellite can. Ryder, you did one hell of a job getting cameras installed in this place. I almost feel like a cheat, taking your money. I spend most of the day just watching the screens, and this lovely lady over here"—he paused to indicate Stephanie—"keeps me fed way better than I tend to feed myself."

"I've been in the nook and checked all the screens myself," Ryder said. "It is a pretty good setup, if I do say so."

"It's fine for you to say so. And also fine that you keep paying me," Arnie said lightly.

"Not a problem," Ryder assured him. "Let's get on in, shall we?"

"I'm just doing my walk-around," Arnie said.

"Thanks," Ryder told him.

"After that, you can find me in my nook."

They went into the house.

Stephanie looked at Casey. "You have an overnight bag. Are you staying here?"

"With your permission, of course. Ryder suggested it made sense."

Stephanie glanced at Ryder but then smiled at Casey. "You really did know my sister."

"I did know her, yes. Not well. But she came to the shop several times. I wouldn't have lied to you."

"No one can lie to a two-year-old and get away with it," Stephanie said lightly. "And, speaking of the two-year-old, it's late. I'm going to get her to bed." Stephanie hesitated and glanced at Casey. "If he brought you here...well, I know my cousin. He's vetted you, and there's a good reason you're here, especially since I'm sure you have your own home."

Casey nodded.

"Okay then, go on up the grand staircase. It's a beautiful house, and I can't tell you how much I hate it. The strangest thing is...neither Anthony nor Lena was into money or material things. And here I am. But whoever did this isn't going to win." She dropped her chin, eyes downcast. "I'm a coward, so I'd consider taking Annette and running, but I'm afraid we'd be hunted down. Annette and I must be here. Especially until..." Her voice trailed, and she turned to Ryder.

"Put the baby to bed," he told her. "We'll talk after."

"I have her crib in my room," Stephanie said. "Right next to my bed."

"Then we'll talk in the morning," Ryder said.

Stephanie nodded and took Annette from Casey.

"Make yourself at home, Casey. Please. The kitchen is wide open. Gail Reeves lives on the property, but she has the old carriage house out back." Stephanie paused. "I don't even let Gail in anymore until she calls and tells me she's ready to come over. Anyway, sorry, I'm talking away. And this kid needs to go down for the night. I'll see you in the morning."

She turned and started for the stairs, but then turned back and looked at Casey.

"You've seen my sister, right? Her spirit or...ghost?"

"I—yes," Casey said.

"And now I've seen her, too, Stephanie," Ryder said. "We are going to solve Lena's murder."

Stephanie smiled. "I know you will. Just do so quickly, please. Okay? I'm going nuts here."

This time, she continued up the stairs.

Ryder looked at Casey.

"Come on up. I'll give you the Blue Room. Goes with your eyes." He winked.

"Great. I'm all into matching," Casey said dryly.

He carried her bag and led the way. The Blue Room was in the west wing, across from another guest room—the Gold Room in his case. All the rooms were named for colors except for the master suite—which had a plaque on it that said: *Master Suite.*

No one was in it now. Stephanie wouldn't sleep where her sister had died.

But Stephanie was in the baby's room, also in the west wing.

He liked being near those he was watching over.

Even with a trusted guard on duty.

Even with the elaborate system he'd installed.

"Blue Room," he said, opening the door and leading Casey in. The carpet and drapes were navy blue, the bed covering a softer pale blue.

"It is—blue," she said.

"I think it's probably comfortable—"

"Oh, no. It's lovely. I was just noting that it is well, blue."

He grinned at her. "Bathroom is right there to the side. The old man had all the old dressing rooms turned into bathrooms. Elijah." He hesitated and shrugged. "He was a good man. Anyway, you're welcome to prowl the kitchen below if you get hungry. I'm across the hall in the Gold Room if you should need anything. Or if you'd like something, I can get it for you now."

"No, I'm going to try to sleep, thanks."

"Okay, then."

He looked at her for a moment. He'd just met her. She'd angered him to no end when he thought her a fraud.

And now...

He liked her. *Really* liked her. And that was...unexpected.

He noticed how her hair fell around her face in soft waves. How her eyes studied everything intensely. She was thoughtful and quick-witted. Smart and intuitive.

And he'd seen her in a bikini. Ryder smiled at the memory.

But he'd put her into extreme danger. Unless she had already done that to herself.

It didn't matter. This was no time for his instinctive sex drive to kick in.

"Good night, then," he said quickly. "Um, just amble down to the kitchen in the morning whenever you like."

"Thank you," she told him.

He smiled and closed the door behind him, hurrying to his room.

He had worried so much when he first arrived. He hadn't wanted to leave Stephanie and the baby alone.

People would know about William Marley's exhumation.

His presence had been required at the cemetery. And before that...

He'd been so angry when Stephanie had thought a quack *medium* had come to her. He'd taken off, trusting in Greg Farley, the morning shift guard, to keep the home safe.

Hovering at the house wouldn't solve anything.

But...

He'd seen one of his prime suspects studying Casey's shop. And there had been someone in the bushes at her home when she was out alone in the pool. She'd known it—and Lena had known it.

And now, he knew what had happened from Lena herself.

He decided to put a call through. He could get help when he needed it.

And he needed it now.

* * * *

The bed was amazingly comfortable. She'd brought her own things, but she felt as if she were staying in a hotel room. Anything anyone might desire was available in the bathroom, from toothpaste to soap, to shampoo, conditioner, and a hairdryer.

She wondered if—in the past—company executives had stayed at the mansion. Or if they were due to come again.

Not anytime soon, she imagined.

Despite the luxury of her accommodations, she lay awake.

She wondered if Lena would show up, but she didn't. Maybe she was as polite in death as she was in life and not about to disturb anyone trying to sleep.

Casey still couldn't believe that she was here. Even after the shock of seeing and accepting Lena Marceau as a ghost, she had never expected a day like today. And the last thing she wanted to do was think about the strange ghost-seeing FBI agent, who had come into her life like an exploding volcano—and become her most curious ally.

As she had become his.

She stared at the dark ceiling, remembering his voice. The way he stood, the way he'd held her when she burst into her apartment building, dripping...

How he hadn't minded giving her a real apology, or the fact that he took her safety so seriously.

She was a link to Lena—and Lena's killer.

Still...

She liked him. Too much. She was thinking about him in many ways...

Too much.

Finally, she turned on the television and fell asleep at last to a rerun of *Cheers*.

She woke late, at least for her. It was almost eight o'clock. For a minute, she blinked and then remembered her surroundings and why she was there. She rose, showered, dug into her little bag, and dressed for the day.

It was still so damned hot. She had brought—ironically, she thought—a blue halter dress and a black sweater to wear when the air-conditioning kicked in.

Jared and Lauren really liked to blast it at the shop.

Ready for the day, she left her room and hurried downstairs to the kitchen, where she found Ryder and Stephanie and the baby.

Annette was in her highchair, playing with her cereal as much as eating it. The highchair was pulled up to a small kitchen table. Stephanie was on one side, Ryder on the other.

Apparently, Annette loved to say, "Hi!" because she greeted Casey with the word and a big smile and then said, "Hi!" again.

"Hi, you," Casey said, ruffling the little girl's hair.

Annette took her hand.

"Good morning. Did you sleep all right?" Stephanie asked her.

"Yes, thank you. The room is lovely."

Ryder was on the phone with someone, and he lifted a hand and gave her a smile, indicating he'd be off soon.

"Coffee?" Stephanie asked.

"I would love some. Can I do anything? You don't need to wait on me."

"No, no—the pot is right there. I'm not much of a cook. I'm afraid breakfast is cereal or toaster waffles."

"Cereal is great, thank you," Casey said.

Her cell phone rang as Stephanie poured her a cup of coffee. She excused herself and dug into her purse for her mobile.

It was Miss Lilly. She winced. She should have told her concerned neighbor that she'd be away.

"I'm so sorry, Miss Lilly. I'm fine. Just staying with a friend."

Ryder had finished his call and was looking at her.

"Oh, don't apologize, darling," Miss Lilly said. "Joe and I are delighted you apparently spent the night with that tall, dark, and devilishly handsome fellow. I've been telling you for ages you can't just work and read and swim. I mean, I love swimming, but—"

Casey wanted to sink under the table. Lilly was speaking loudly, and Casey was sure Ryder could hear every word.

"I mean, you're a young, lovely thing. Sweet as molasses, too. Oh, wait, not sticky sweet. I mean, you have a mind on you, and you're smart, too. But everyone needs a sex life," Lilly said with a giggle. "Even oldsters."

Casey knew she visibly winced.

"Joe and I...we just wanted to make sure you were okay."

"I'm fine, Miss Lilly. I may be away for a few days."

"Ah, you little scamp. You have fun! Life is short. You'll have to tell me all about it when I see you next."

"Um...sure, of course. Miss Lilly, I have to get back to—"

"Oh, get back to it. I didn't mean to interrupt."

Ryder was laughing. The baby was giggling, and even Stephanie must have heard Lilly because she was smiling, too.

"I'm so sorry," Casey said, explaining to Stephanie. "One of my neighbors. She's a sweetheart, worrying about me, really. And I...I'm sorry."

"Hey, what are you sorry for? It's nice that a neighbor cares," Stephanie said.

Ryder had a smirk on his face. He passed her the box of cereal as Stephanie set down a bowl and a cup of coffee.

"It is nice," he said. "She apparently likes us both. And me, from just meeting her at her main door."

Stephanie smiled and joined them again as she looked at Casey. "Have you seen Lena this morning? She must have liked you very much. I mean, Annette likes you."

"I haven't seen her this morning. But...I know how she loved you and appreciates you," Casey said earnestly.

"Well, I hope she comes to the house sometime," Stephanie said softly. "I want her to know how much I love her—will always love her. She was my only sibling. It feels like a part of me was cut away. I'm so grateful I have Annette. And so scared."

"Stephanie—" Ryder began.

They were cut short by the buzzer.

"That's Jackson," Ryder said, pushing his chair back. "Excuse me. I'll just let him in."

He left the kitchen to answer the intercom and open the gate.

"Jackson?" Casey said to Stephanie.

"Jackson Crow, Ryder's field director. He's going to hang with the baby and me today."

"Oh," Casey said and smiled. "Um, nice."

Stephanie laughed. "Jackson is great. He's six-foot-something of Native American and Irish and incredibly good-looking. And married. Very married, with two kids, and a spectacular wife who manages and juggles the Krewe of Hunters. You'd be amazed by some of the strange activities that go on around the country." She was quiet for a minute. "And the departed who stay because they need help or need to help someone else. Like Lena," she added softly. She squared her shoulders then and stood ready to meet the newcomer.

Annette started to cry, wanting out of her chair. Casey instinctively went to get her and remembered that Stephanie was her guardian. She asked, "May I?"

"Oh, please. I miss her little daycare most of all in this insanity of being so careful. She needs more fun than I can really supply."

Casey rescued the baby, who wanted to run out of the kitchen and to the door. She moved like lightning, but Casey kept up.

Ryder introduced her to Jackson Crow, who seemed to be everything Stephanie had said.

He was also good with children, saying, "Hi," to Annette in answer to her every "Hi!"

He studied Casey and was friendly and cordial, thanking her for being there.

"What a way to come into this," he said. "But then, it never is easy."

"We're going to head to the French Quarter," Ryder told him. "Casey opens the shop at ten, so I guess we need to get going. Bobby O'Hara is in the library now, keeping an eye on the video screens. Come in there for just a minute. I'll introduce you."

Annette raced after Ryder and Jackson, and Stephanie and Casey raced after Annette. Annette ran to the corner to play with some books. Jackson and Casey were both introduced to Bobby O'Hara, another of Ryder's old friends. Bobby, in contrast to Arnie Benson, had a full head of white hair and a cavalier mustache.

Casey greeted him pleasantly, but as she spoke, her eyes wandered around the handsome library before stopping to hear what was being said.

There was a row of pictures on the wall.

"Are you all right, Casey?" Ryder asked.

"Um, sorry. Who are those men?" she asked.

"They're all on the board of directors," Stephanie supplied.

"Why?" Ryder asked Casey.

"I—I've seen them. Two of them, anyway. They've been in my shop."

Chapter 6

Casey stared at the pictures.

Yes, she had seen two of the men. She walked toward the photos on the side wall. A desk sat against that wall, while the rest of the walls were filled with shelves and books—other than the security nook Ryder had created.

Above the desk hung a sign that read: *Past and present leaders of Marceau Industries Incorporated. We thank them.*

"They came to the shop when? Who came? Which men?"

Casey pointed to two of the pictures. One was of an older man, another of a man about forty. They hadn't come in together. They had come in at different times.

"That's Barton Quincy, the new CEO. And that's his assistant, Larry Swenson," Ryder said. He caught her gently by the shoulders and turned her around to face him.

"Casey, when did they come in? Did they see you...with Lena?"

She shook her head. "They were both in before I saw Lena in the shop. I mean, Lena's ghost. They were in that night, though. They both bought a few things and talked about a reading."

Ryder released her and then paused. His eyes were on the wall, focused on a section that included past leaders of the company.

"Ryder?" she said.

He pointed to another picture. "That's William Marley. The man we had exhumed, whose cremains are being studied in Mississippi."

"Oh," she murmured.

"We're still waiting on results, but tests take time, especially when you're dealing with a corpse that has been..."

"Baking in the Louisiana sun," Stephanie supplied.

"To put it gently, yes," Ryder said. "Jackson—"

"Angela has done extensive background checks on every man on the board," Jackson said. "Nothing in the paperwork helps. Justin Marceau was busted as a kid for pot. Larry Swenson had a lot of parking tickets. Expensive, but a far cry from premeditated murder. Harry Miller didn't even have a traffic infraction against him. After a month of searching, the only thing she could discover was the unusual way that William Marley died. Suffering from a sudden heart attack without having any problems with heart disease at all."

"Stephanie, I think you need to call a board meeting," Ryder said.

"But I—I don't know anything. I approve or deny decisions as the baby's trust officer, but I don't know much. I was never a businessperson. The only thing I ever knew was that both Anthony and Lena were passionate about keeping the price of life-saving drugs down as much as possible. And I believed it was all just a formality, naming me as Annette's legal guardian. Anthony and Lena were young. I never thought it could really happen. I heard Anthony arguing with one of the men once. I don't even know which one. He said that, yes, you had to pay staff and have laboratories, but they didn't need to make a lot of money off prescriptions that people need for heart conditions or diabetes or other such diseases. Anthony said he wasn't going to make money off the lives of others."

"It's okay. You'll just call the meeting to make sure the company can make money in other ways. Slight increases on their organic vitamins and other such items," Ryder said. "That will be it. The meeting will be to make everyone understand that you—as Annette's guardian—will veto any suggestion of a price increase in new or old drugs. Elijah was a smart old geezer. He created the board but kept ultimate control on all aspects. And that authority has now passed down to you and Annette. You can just say you're calling the meeting to make sure everyone knows the direction the company will be taking, and Marceau Industries Incorporated will honor the wishes of Elijah, Anthony, and Lena."

"Okay, but I don't think I can call a meeting for today. I believe Justin is in Biloxi, speaking with a chemist they want to hire," Stephanie said. "And I have no idea if the other guys are in the office or not."

"Tomorrow will be fine. For now, I'll head to the French Quarter with Casey, and Jackson will stay here and get some work done," Ryder said. He glanced at Jackson, and knew the man would have Angela dig deeper into every possible—and impossible—resource to find out more about Barton Quincy and Larry Swenson."

Casey looked at them all with a frown. "Wouldn't Justin be the one to benefit if...if he were the one who—?"

"Was around if something happened to me and Annette?" Stephanie said. "No, that's the odd thing. If something happens to both of us and there are only four board members left, it's an equal split. Elijah just wasn't close to Justin. When Justin asked for a job, he gave it to him. But he only got a position because he was a Marceau, and Elijah couldn't let a family member have nothing. So, he worked with Justin, and Justin *does* have a charming personality. It turned out he wasn't so bad when it came to marketing, advertising, and especially, personal appearances," she finished.

"I need to get to the shop," Casey murmured. "I open today."

"Okay, we're out," Ryder said.

"And we'll be on it from any angle we can find," Jackson assured him.

Ryder looked at Casey. "Time to get you to work."

"You're coming to work with me?"

He paused to let her see the seriousness of his words. "I'll be in or near the shop all day."

Her eyes rounded at his unspoken message. "You think someone might come after me. In a shop in the French Quarter?"

"I think someone will be watching you, and I want to see who. Also, with the meeting tomorrow, we may get something. And we should get some lab results back from the M.E. over in Mississippi. So for now...I'm your constant companion," Ryder said.

He was curious to see if she would object.

She didn't. She just glanced at her watch.

"Then we should get going."

* * * *

It was interesting, Casey thought, bringing Ryder into the shop with her, especially after what had happened the morning before. In the hours since, she had gotten to know him...

And it was strange that in the short time they'd spent together, she somehow felt ridiculously close to him.

Of course, he might end up saving her life. He was security.

But he was also more.

She really hadn't wanted to like him. But she did. And she sure as hell hadn't wanted to find him intriguing, compelling, and attractive.

Sexually attractive.

But she did.

She'd had a few weird dreams. They should have been about ghosts...being haunted.

They weren't. Her dreams hadn't been horror stories at all. Rather, they were fantasies. There had been something like an old disco ball sending rays of color everywhere, and she and Ryder had been dancing. He had been giving her that strange smile of his as if they shared something unique and special. It was an incredible secret and a bond that went deeper than any other could go. She felt the strength of him in every movement. In their dance, he pulled her close, his eyes both tender and aflame, and she thought they'd come closer and closer until... She had woken up.

Now, she was the first to arrive at the shop. Once she opened, Ryder took a seat in one of the comfortable chairs by the coffee and tea service until Jared and Lauren arrived.

He stood to greet them. "Uh—hi."

"Hi," the two said in unison, staring from him to Casey.

"It's all right," Casey said quickly. "We had a chance to speak yesterday. Ryder is with the FBI." She hesitated. "He and Lena Marceau were cousins."

Jared still looked protective and fierce, as much as someone who was almost a throwback to a love-all hippie could.

Lauren seemed curious and wary.

"And how does that affect you or the shop in any way?" Lauren asked. She looked at Ryder. "I have a cell phone on me, and I can hit *emergency call* with the twitch of my hand."

Casey laughed and went over to hug her and then Jared.

"What's going on? Really?" Jared asked.

"Lena Marceau was in the store several times," Casey explained. "We...we wound up having some serious conversations. I'm good with kids, so...we talked. She talked about her husband and about it being crazy having so much money. She didn't believe her husband fell off a building, and she was frightened for herself and Annette. I told her to talk to the police. She told *me* she had planned to. I was sad when I heard she'd killed herself. You know Jennie was convinced she saw ghosts at the cemetery. Then...I went to see Stephanie Harrow, the baby's guardian. And Ryder thought that..."

"I thought she was a sham, just tormenting Stephanie. Or worse," Ryder said. "I thought she might be part of something horribly devious like getting rid of Stephanie and the baby, too."

"But..." Lauren spoke and then looked confused. "Hey, I'm not FBI or anything—art major here—but even I know you look at the person who would benefit."

"There are four people who would benefit," Ryder explained. "But there's also murder for hire. Whoever is doing all this is in for the long-haul. But we discovered that another person in the higher-up section of the company might not have died of a simple heart attack. And I think someone started watching Casey. So...I'm here for a bit."

Lauren and Jared looked at each other.

"Well, we'll be nice and safe," Lauren said.

"Not that we've had trouble," Jared put in.

"But you never know. New Orleans is not without crime," Lauren said, but then she frowned. "You can't just arrest the four people?"

Ryder smiled at her. "Well, there's the Constitution. Innocent until proven guilty. And proving anyone guilty in this...it hasn't been easy. Anyway, I'll be in here for part of the day, and scouring the area the other parts. If I can help anyone in any way, just let me know."

"Nice. Thank you," Lauren said.

"I'm going to hang a few large canvases if you want to pitch in," Jared said.

"Sure."

A woman came in to browse the tee shirts, souvenirs, and jewelry. Casey spoke to her, showing her which goods were local, and explaining what some of the symbolic jewelry meant. Lauren spoke to another woman about a sketch of Jackson Square.

Ryder worked on the canvases with Jared. The two talked easily. She heard Ryder tell Jared at one point, "Yeah, I have a degree. Criminology. I'm afraid I haven't an artistic bone in my body, but that doesn't mean I don't love art and music."

"Everyone has music," Jared assured him. "It's in the body, the blood, the mind, and the soul."

Ryder's phone rang, and he excused himself, walking outside and down the block. Casey watched him go.

Lauren was next to her where she stood behind the counter.

"Okay...nice!"

"Yes. I mean, it turns out he was just really upset. I guess I don't blame him. I suppose it was just something eating at me. We do have a shop where I do readings, and people often think that means you assume you're something you can't be. Anyway, Ryder was protecting his cousin, Stephanie Harrow, Lena Marceau's sister. And—"

"I'm glad he turned out to be nice. Because he is...well, he's employed, for one."

Lauren had been engaged for a while to a man who turned out to be using her for room and board.

"He's employed, yes," Casey said and laughed.

Lauren grinned. "And he has a damned good body."

"He seems to be in shape."

"Great face. Those eyes of his..."

Casey knew where this was going but smiled at her friend. "He is nice-looking."

"And he likes you."

"He's protecting me," she made clear.

"No, he *likes* you. You can see it in his eyes."

Casey thought about the short time they'd spent together. Their chemistry and conversation. The way he was not only with her but with his cousin and little Annette. He was kind, with a protective streak a mile wide. She knew it was fast, but she trusted what her feelings were telling her. "And I like him."

"Hmmm…" Lauren mused. "He's probably honorable and ethical and all that."

"I imagine he has some good qualities." Casey chuckled.

"Men like that don't come around every day, Casey," Lauren said, a seriousness replacing the levity of their conversation. "And you never just go out, which means the last time you were with someone was when you were seeing Sam Tourneau. He was nice enough, employed, good-looking..."

"And he only loved football." Casey remembered the sting of that breakup. "I like football. But I also enjoy music and my friends and...books and art and things besides sports. But we're still friends."

"Right. And he was a decent guy. But you don't go out a lot. I think this guy is cool, and you should get something going."

"He lives in Virginia or somewhere in that area," Casey reminded Lauren.

"Okay. So maybe he goes away in a bit. Seize the moment, my friend.

I know what you should do if you worry about where things might go."
Lauren's eyes widened. "Go mad for a few days. Don't let it get awkward.
He's an agent. A guy on the move. So, premeditated sex."

"What?" Casey almost choked on her laughter.

"Just agree to sex, sex, and nothing but sex." Lauren giggled.

"I think you're mixing up your courtyard dramas." Casey rolled her
eyes.

"I'm just talking about being upfront and honest. You like him. He
likes you. Birds do it, bees do it... Have a thing while he's here."

"Oh, Lauren."

Casey hadn't realized Jared was standing nearby until she heard him
laugh. "I like it! That may be my line. If Lauren would just be a good wing
woman, I may try it on the hot girl playing the washboard at Pete's one of
these days. Premeditated sex."

Casey groaned and was grateful when the shop door opened. A few
members from a local retirees' club came in. They chatted, and then one
turned to Jared and asked, "Where's our song?"

"Your song? Oh, you want your song," Jared said. He looked at
Casey and Lauren. "Ready, ladies? This is one of our finest harmonies."

Casey winced inwardly. Their favorite song was from Blue Oyster
Cult. *Don't Fear the Reaper.*

They did do excellent harmony with it.

But Casey didn't get a chance to answer. Jared had already gotten his
guitar and started strumming. She and Lauren were behind the counter.
Lauren flung an arm around Casey's shoulders and smiled, and they began
the song.

Casey hoped Lena Marceau would not pick this time to come by.

Luckily, she didn't see the ghost. Ryder, however, returned at the end
of the tune, and while he had a strange expression on his face, he clapped
along with the retirees. The group chatted and talked, and a couple of
their members bought a few pieces.

The store emptied, and Ryder looked at them, moving his gaze from
one to the other.

"Hm, do you people have a lunch or dinner break? Or whatever meal
it is one has in the afternoon?"

"Oh, yeah, we cover for one another," Lauren said. "Why don't you
and Casey go on out and get something? I had a big breakfast."

"I didn't," Jared said and then gulped as Lauren nudged him in the
ribcage.

"But I'm not hungry yet," he added quickly. "You two go. And get back. Then, we'll go."

"Okay with you?" Ryder asked Casey.

"Sure."

"She has something to ask you. Or suggest," Lauren said.

Casey cast Lauren a scathing glare. Lauren smiled.

They started out of the store, and Ryder asked, "What would you like? We're in the French Quarter. Most places are wonderful."

"I'm not... I don't care. I'm not that hungry. I'm actually a little on edge." She looked at him searchingly. "Have you seen Lena?"

He shook his head. "Not today. I believe she'll find us by tonight. We know she's been to the house. She sees Annette that way."

"Of course," Casey murmured.

"So, what did you want to ask or suggest?" He looked at her with concern.

She shook her head. "That was just Lauren being silly."

"She's talented. There are wonderful artists working all over this city. It's a magnet for creative types, I think. But Lauren's work has something special in it. Heart. She has a true feel for everything unique and wonderful about this city."

"Did you spend a lot of time here?"

"I did. Growing up. I was born in Gretna. Anyway, food. I *am* hungry."

"Okay. Wherever. What about your call? The one you left the store to take."

"Ah, that." He smiled tightly. "That was my ticket into serious delving. The medical examiner from Mississippi called." He winced. "I was there for the exhumation, and I have to say, I think I'm going to be cremated from the get-go. William Marley was embalmed, and the work was good. So, he decayed in the heat, but...there were remains. Enough for the M.E. to discover there had been a massive dose of cocaine in his system. He was well-known and had never been a drug user in life. At this point, the M.E. couldn't find the delivery system, but he's convinced the heart attack was brought on by the cocaine."

"So, he *was* murdered."

"Yes, and Jackson is going through the proper channels to see that the investigation into Lena's death is reopened with the FBI. With me heading up the investigation."

"I'm happy for you. But where do you go from here?"

"I have a friend locally who was one of the detectives on the original case. I'm going to bring him back in. And after Stephanie's meeting tomorrow, I'm going to go after the board of directors one by one. Nobody else benefits from these deaths. I wish it was as easy as Lauren's suggestion that we just arrest them all, or that Lena could just appear in front of a judge and demand they all stand trial. But we need evidence."

"How did he get into the house—whoever the man in all the black clothing was?" Casey asked.

"Whoever got in knew the security code for the gate and the front door. Either that, or Gail Reeves let him in. But she was at her book club meeting. Several people vouched for that. Muriel's."

"Pardon?"

"For lunch. Muriel's, Jackson Square. I've always loved it."

"Fine with me."

They were about a block or so away after having ambled somewhat aimlessly.

Casey had always loved Muriel's, too. The place was rumored to have several resident ghosts, mostly past owners of the property. There had been a building at the location soon after the city was founded, *La Nouvelle Orleans*. The great mansion that had stood on the spot had been horribly damaged in the great fire that swept the city in 1788, though it had been rebuilt. The property was still prime real estate—caddy-corner from Jackson Square.

"You know they have séance rooms," Ryder said dryly.

"And they really have seances." She smiled.

They were only interested in eating today, and a friendly hostess quickly gave them a table.

They were served iced tea while their entrees were prepared. As they waited, Ryder leaned close and said, "I really am sorry."

"You don't have to keep apologizing. I understand."

"Okay."

"Good."

"I was wrong about you."

"I guess I was wrong about you also. Too bad you don't live here. At some point, I could have taken you to see some amazing bands. Jared is friends with just about every musician in the city."

"Maybe I'll stick around long enough for you to take me out."

She grinned. "Are you picking up our late lunch or early dinner?" she asked.

"I am."

"Okay, then. I'll take you out."

"Sounds good. We'll be almost like a couple."

He was still close, and she could see a light in his eyes, both teasing and serious. "I was really wrong. I like you and admire you," he said softly.

"Um—thank you."

He leaned back, smiling. "You could tell me how much you like and admire me, too."

She laughed softly. "I do like and admire you, even knowing what an ass you can be. But that's okay. I understand." She took a sip of her tea.

"So," Casey murmured awkwardly, "what's your life like when you're not chasing down devious killers?"

"The Krewe is an amazing unit. According to the papers that define us, we go in when there are unusual aspects to a case. Adam and Jackson have drawn together an incredible group that has gotten larger over the years. We have our own separate headquarters, an array of forensic investigators, and some of the best computer forensic people to be found."

"Your life is work?"

He shrugged. "A lot of us are friends. We know and understand each other. We go to ballgames. Adam owns a non-profit theater. Several spouses and significant others actually work there. We see lots of wonderful shows. We go to concerts, movies...and we have a Friday night poker game for whoever shows up."

"Nice. I thought you were going to say you worked all the time."

"I do work a lot. But you work all the time, too."

"Work is fun. Lauren is an amazing artist, and I help with her projects. And we have a great time with Jared. He has some original work, and Lauren and I are going to help out when he records."

"Are those two together?"

"No. They're just best friends. We all are. We decided in college that we'd never screw it all up by dating each other."

"So none of you is married or about to be married?" He leaned in closer.

"Are you?" she volleyed back.

"No."

"Why not?"

"What?"

It was his turn to back off. Then he shrugged. "I came close. But...yeah. Work. I should say it was never going to work. She's a good woman. We're still casual friends. But she was..."

"Clingy?" Casey suggested as he looked for a word.

"Yeah. I'm a decent guy. If I were going to do something, I'd just say it. But she was suspicious every time I got a call in the night, and I don't believe in a life without trust."

"I'm with you there. I never came close to marriage. I guess I tend to back off quickly, and Lauren complains I don't give things a chance. But there needs to be some common ground when you're looking at long-term." She winced slightly. "Well, anyway...the food is great, as always. I should get back."

"I'm going to go in with you and then head back out to the street."

"Okay. You really think someone is watching the shop?"

"I really do. You already told me you had seen both Barton Quincy and Larry Swenson in A Beautiful Mind."

"But that was before Lena came to me that night."

"I'm guessing they knew Lena had been there before."

"But just because she was there—"

"You don't claim to be a medium. But you *do* read tea leaves and the tarot. If they knew she had been to your shop, they might have been trying to find out if she'd come to you with her accusation that someone helped Anthony off that building. And if so, even though it's a bit of a stretch...maybe they were trying to make sure she didn't give you information from the beyond."

"Wait. You think our killer believes in the occult? Even I didn't believe that a ghost delivering a message was possible until Lena appeared."

"Either the killer believes or doesn't want to take any chances with loose ends." He smiled at her. "But don't worry, I promise you...until I know you're safe, I'll be close to you at all times."

Casey smiled weakly. She wasn't sure how close she wanted him to be. The more they were together, the more she felt the strength of simple attraction.

No...

Not simple. He had proven to be decent, ethical, and even courteous. There was no denying his appearance, the shoulders, the slim hips. His long legs, great face...

She couldn't shake Lauren's words.

Premeditated sex!

But she couldn't see herself just suggesting that to him since neither of them had anything else going on. *How about some recreational sex?*

"Ah, yeah." She cleared her throat. "We'd better get going."

He paid the tab, and they left, walking side by side the few blocks back to the shop.

Their arms occasionally brushed as they walked. He caught her hand to steer her to his side when a kid on a bicycle almost ran them off the sidewalk. It was good to feel his hand surrounding hers.

And to wonder just how good it would feel elsewhere...

Chapter 7

Ryder left Casey to wander, moving across the street and then up the other way.

The concept that someone was watching her at the shop might be crazy, but if Barton Quincy and Larry Swenson had been in her shop, it gave credence to the idea that someone was suspicious of her.

Finding out who among his list of suspects might believe in the occult would be an interesting aspect to the case.

He had wandered down two blocks, pretending to look in shop windows, when he saw a woman entering Casey's store—Gail Reeves, the Marceau's housekeeper.

He didn't think Casey had met the woman when she was at the house. She'd seen Stephanie that day, and only Stephanie. Gail had been out, or so he thought, and he had been with Annette.

He strode back, wondering if he should go in. He might as well. Gail knew Casey had come to the house. Stephanie had gone on about being accosted by the city's *mystics*, so Gail knew about Casey.

Which meant, she must know he was watching over Casey and the shop.

He strode toward it, pausing when his phone rang.

It was Braxton.

"Hello, Detective Wild."

"Hello, Special Agent McKinley. I guess I'm working for you."

"Working *with* me," Ryder said.

"Apparently, they're quietly reopening cases—William Marley, Anthony Marceau, and Lena Marceau."

"Someone helped William Marley have that heart attack," Ryder said.

"Evidently. Can you tell me what's new?"

"I'm on the street. Jackson Crow is in the city, but we'll be calling on your people for help. Of course, we have our field office here, but we want the NOPD to be equal partners with us in finding out what the hell is going on."

"Right. I don't know—"

"I'm on St. Anne. There's a coffee shop—"

"Thirty minutes?"

"Sounds about right."

Ryder ended the conversation in time to see Gail Reeves leaving Casey's store. He walked in a few minutes later.

"Gail was just here," Casey said.

"I saw."

"She said she'd heard about me and mentioned she loves shops like this and knew I had to be good if Lena came here. She wanted to set up a tarot reading. I told her Lena had not come in for a reading. And she said Lena had mentioned the shop and how much she loved it and how she felt an affinity toward me."

"Ah."

"So?"

"I'm not sure. But that's interesting. I'm going to walk over to the coffee shop and meet up with Braxton Wild, the detective called in when Lena died. He'll be working with us on this. I need to bring him up to speed. I can see the shop from there."

"Thanks," she told him, smiling as a woman walked into the store.

"Jennie! Hey, I thought you were on vacation," Casey said. The woman was a customer Casey obviously knew well.

She was older, slim, and attractive, and made no pretense of doing anything but staring at Ryder.

"Hi!" she said, ignoring Casey's question.

"Hi." Ryder smiled at her. "Ryder McKinley," he told her.

"I like it," she said, looking at Casey. Then she added, "Oh, sorry. Jennie Sanders. I love this place—and Casey. She's the best. Did you come for a reading?" she asked him.

"I just love the shop, too," he said lightly. "And Casey, of course. She *is* the best. I'll see you in a bit, Casey. I'm off for coffee."

"You aren't from around here, are you?"

"Actually? Originally from Gretna. Nice to meet you, Jennie. Later, Casey."

He still heard the woman as he walked out of the store.

"Good thing I came in. I did say you might not be here if someone tall, dark, and dangerously handsome walked in. And did you hear? It almost sounded like he said he loves you. What? Don't give me that look. Oh, Casey, I hope you jumped all over him."

The door closed behind him, and he laughed, surprised that he could. It seemed his every waking minute had been bound by tension for too long...

And then Casey had come into his life. She wasn't really *in* his life. More, she was letting him into hers. For now. But...

Braxton must have been in the French Quarter or at least near it. He was already waving to Ryder from a table at the coffee shop. It seemed he'd ordered. Ryder could see he had gotten two large cups of coffee, and Ryder knew one was for him.

He joined the detective, sliding into a chair that allowed him to easily see Casey's shop.

"I'm glad you're in charge of this thing," Braxton told him. "Because I don't know where to go. We questioned the men on the company's board of directors—especially Justin, since he is a Marceau, but he doesn't benefit any more than any of the others. He was not a beloved grandson like Anthony. I checked that out. He didn't seem bitter about it and said he hadn't cared about it or even Elijah much when he was younger. He was just glad his name had given him a position since he hadn't been stellar in any career he undertook himself. We questioned Gail Reeves, too. And, yes, the woman was with her book club. How are you going to get anywhere from here? You said Jackson is here, but can you really babysit Stephanie and Annette for the rest of your life? And even if you could...there could be that one slip, one moment..."

"I could use some help keeping an eye on the shop right there," Ryder said, pointing across the street.

"*A Beautiful Mind,*" Braxton said. "Someone with a beautiful mind did all this?" he asked dryly.

Ryder grimaced.

"Okay, my humor isn't great."

"Before she died, Lena visited the shop several times. She said something to the owner, Casey Nicholson. Casey finally went to Stephanie's house, feeling like a fool but determined to let Stephanie know Lena had been afraid her husband's death had been no accident. Anyway, I found out Barton Quincy and Larry Swenson were in the shop, too. Separately, just looking. I don't think they were shopping. I think they were trying to find out if Casey knew anything."

"So, both men are guilty."

"Maybe."

"Conspiracy theory?"

"Braxton, we know William Marley was helped into a heart attack. We know something happened. Maybe Larry was just doing something for Quincy. Perhaps they're both involved. Didn't the board members give the board alibis when the investigation began?"

Braxton nodded. "But how...?"

"I don't know. We need to find out. Anyway, I need to be at the board meeting Stephanie is calling for tomorrow. So, I need you on the shop."

"All right. On it. What about the baby?"

Ryder grinned. "Jackson is great with kids. He has some of his own."

"All right," Braxton repeated.

"The shop opens at ten. Casey works with two friends from her college days. It's pretty cool. The female is an artist—a damned good one. The male with them is a musician, and they all perform in the shop when customers ask them to. You'll be fine."

"I'll be fine. But you don't have anything else?"

"Actually, I do. I think someone was trying to get to Casey Nicholson the other night. I couldn't catch him. He was wearing black and crawling around in the building's shrubbery."

"You couldn't catch him? You're slipping, my friend."

Ryder gave him a dry smile. "Oh, I will catch him. Trust me. I will catch him."

* * * *

The day passed quickly. Not a bad one. Customers came in and out. Casey and Lauren sang with Jared a few times, and she convinced Jennie that Ryder was a visiting friend, and that she wasn't being whisked away. Said he'd be going back to work in Virginia.

He hadn't stated his title when he introduced himself. She didn't want to go into it all with Jennie anyway, so she was as casual as she could be.

"Don't let that one get away!" Jennie told her.

Casey smiled and patiently explained, "I don't have him, so he can't get away."

"If you don't have him, do something. You should have him," Jennie told her. "Anyway, I just stopped by because my car needed a little work. I'm leaving in the morning."

"That's good. Family is good, Jennie. Give us a call and let us know you got there okay."

"Ah, you're sweet. I will do so," she promised.

Then she was gone.

Lauren and Jared returned, and friends from one of Lauren's art classes came in while Jared was talking to a friend he knew from a band.

Restless, Casey glanced at Jared and said, "Running out for just a minute."

She wasn't sure Ryder would appreciate it if she honed-in on his meeting at the coffee shop, but she just needed out of the shop for a minute.

Being anxious was something that seemed to grow within her.

She had barely started down the street when someone slipped out of a narrow alleyway between the storefronts, taking her hand and drawing her back, whispering quickly at the same time. "It's me. It's okay. But come back here."

Ryder. He had her hard against him. She turned in his hold, confused. He was looking down the street. She saw one of the men she had seen before in her shop. She remembered the pictures in the Marceau house library.

Larry Swenson. She twisted in Ryder's arms, so close that she was looking up into his face. He looked down at her. It was almost as if they were in a lover's embrace. He grimaced, then glanced back down the street before looking into her eyes again. He touched her face gently. "I'm sorry. I want to see what he's up to."

She nodded, staring back at him.

Larry Swenson paused in front of A Beautiful Mind.

He looked in the shop, frowned, and moved on.

"Go back in. Do you mind? Braxton is watching the place. I want to follow Swenson."

She nodded.

"Quickly, okay?"

She nodded again. Then, he was gone, long strides taking him behind the man who had looked into the shop.

She hurried back as she had promised.

The afternoon sun was starting to set when Ryder arrived back at six.

"Hey, girls, get out of here," Jared commanded. "My night. And, Casey, you lucky devil, you're back on the late shift tomorrow."

"All right, then," she said, glancing at Ryder. He hadn't said anything about his excursion following after Larry Swenson.

"Yep, I'm getting my things," Lauren said. Then she added, "Hey, Casey. Don't forget, Miss Lilly's granddaughter's group is coming in tomorrow," Lauren reminded her.

"I won't forget."

Casey noted that Ryder had been talking to Jared, and both were laughing.

"What's up?" she asked, but Jared waved a hand in the air and bid them goodnight. They waved goodbye to Lauren at the door and then started to Ryder's car.

"What happened with Swenson?" she asked.

"He stopped on the next block and made a phone call. I couldn't get close enough to hear without being seen, but he looked at the shop the whole time he talked. He had to have reported he didn't see you in there."

"I could have been in the back in my reading room."

"True. The thing is, it hasn't been happenstance or simple shopping trips. Larry Swenson has an interest in the shop. And you. And he called someone else to report."

"Do you think he knows you're watching over it—and me?"

"Maybe. But Braxton and his people will be watching tomorrow; I'll be at the board meeting with Stephanie."

"So, now—"

"Now, we wait until tomorrow."

They reached his car. As they got in and he pulled out into traffic, Casey remembered she had a long and busy day coming up.

"So, since we're on hold, may we drop by my apartment? I'd like to pick up one of my books."

He arched a brow at her. "You've seen the library at the Marceau house."

"A particular book," she told him. "I'm giving a speech tomorrow to a group of school kids."

He smiled. "Sure."

He was silent then, but it looked as if he were inwardly laughing about something.

"What? What were you and Jared laughing about?" Casey asked.

He shrugged. But he was...smirking.

"What?" she prodded.

He glanced her way and then shook his head before laughing out loud.

"Premeditated sex," he told her.

"Oh, God!" She groaned.

"It's okay. I told him not to worry. I haven't known you long, but it's been long enough to know you'd feel horribly uncomfortable in Stephanie's house, so...no premeditation."

On the one hand, she was mortified. On the other...

She remembered the way his eyes had roamed over her. And the feel of his hand as he touched her cheek. The thrill she felt at even the simple brush of his arm. The strong feel of his body against hers.

"You're right."

He nodded.

She took a deep breath for courage and spoke while looking straight ahead. "But we are going by my apartment."

He glanced her way, arching a brow.

"Premeditated sex?" he asked her.

She looked at him and saw the intensity in his eyes. "What do you think about the idea?" she asked softly.

"Wow."

"Is that a...?"

"I'm all into that kind of premeditation, Casey." His voice had deepened, and his fingers tightened on the steering wheel. But then he seemed to force himself to relax. "I mean, Jared made me laugh, telling me about Lauren's terminology, and I never would have presumed anything. You must have some idea how attractive you are, which has nothing to do with the fact I really do like and admire you." He licked his lips and turned to pin her with his gaze. "But the idea is beyond appealing."

She thought over all she'd been through the last few days. The death of a friend, the possibility of murder, the fear of being targeted. "We don't know where we'll be tomorrow, Ryder. Which is fine with me. I mean, we'll both be in New Orleans, but—"

"We have no guarantees," he said.

Casey looked at him then said softly, "If I've learned anything from all this, none of us even has a guarantee there will be a tomorrow." She winced. "I didn't say that to be hurtful in any way—"

They had reached her neighborhood, if not her building. He pulled the car off the road, reached over, touched her face, and kissed her.

"No guarantees," he whispered. "And life is beautiful. I would like to experience it with you tonight, Casey. Intimately."

She smiled, touching his face, letting her fingers trace the fine contours of his cheekbones, and then running a fingertip lightly over his lips.

"We should really get a room." He smiled.

"I have a room," she breathed.

"We should really get in your room."

"Drive."

He chuckled and drove the rest of the way to her place. He parked, and they got out quickly, Casey reaching for her keys as they did so. She opened the main door.

Miss Lilly was there, and they both came to a dead halt.

"Hello. Lovely to see you both. Casey, I wasn't sure—"

"I'm just stopping by for some things..."

"And I have some calls to make. Important business calls. I can't be disturbed, I'm afraid. We may be a while. Right, Casey?"

"Yes, we may be here a while. But I will be spending the night out again."

"Wonderful!" Lilly said, clapping her hands together. "I'm so delighted to see such lovely young people together. But I wanted to remind you about the children tomorrow."

"I'm all set, Miss Lilly. They'll get their speech."

"Great. Well then, you two go on," Miss Lilly said, turning to head back to her apartment. But she called out to Casey, beckoning to her.

"Honey, don't you read too much or let him work too long. Hang on to that one. I mean, you need to make the most of your time, if you understand me."

Casey smiled. "Thank you."

"And don't worry, you won't be disturbed."

Casey gave the woman a weak smile. As she returned to Ryder and opened the door to her place, she murmured, "Well, that was a surprise to put a stop to—"

She'd opened the door and started through. He moved her forward more quickly, closed the door, and then spun them and pressed her against it.

"No," he murmured. "There are no stops to premeditated sex."

His body leaned hard against hers. The kiss then was nothing like the tender and soft exploration in the car earlier. Ridiculously hot and wet, tongues battling, their hands fumbling with each other at first.

"The bedroom's upstairs," she said when their lips parted.

"I remember." He moved back, his smile now beautiful and seductive.

But he paused to make sure the door was bolted. As he did so, Casey turned and raced up the stairs. He was right behind her. He caught her inside the bedroom, flinging them to the bed together, where they laughed for a moment. Then their laughter faded as they looked at one another.

When they kissed again, the passion of the kiss seemed to radiate and take hold. Shifting, they began to disrobe, and then they were laughing again as they tried to help one another, pausing for Ryder to put his holster and gun aside, then falling upon each other once more. Rolling, lips touching body parts as they were bared, until they were naked at last. He was above her, looking down into Casey's eyes. They kissed, and then his lips traveled the length of her as her fingertips played over his shoulders and back, soft brushes that teased and evoked. Until she rose against him, caressing, kissing, and discovering his body as he had hers. Eventually, they turned again, kissed some more, teased and caressed and seduced and enchanted one another with every brush of their fingers and lips until they came together at last.

Life was beautiful. Being together like this was part of what could be amazing between human beings. Casey briefly thought the future didn't matter. They had bonded in their brief time together, and this...between them...was somehow right. She would never regret this time.

They moved, tossed, arched, writhed, and a rhythm rose and fell between them, becoming sweetly frantic and urgent. Then the world seemed to explode, and it *was* beautiful. As if honeyed crystals filled the night air around Casey. They stilled and lay together, entwined, touching, breathing, just holding tight.

"Casey," Ryder murmured softly.

Suddenly, she was afraid. This had been her choice. She didn't want the night marred by any regrets or worries on his part.

She leaned against his chest and teased lightly, "Premeditated sex. Wow. I really liked it."

He smiled. "Liked? I loved it. I loved it so much, I'm willing to take a chance and go for it again."

She laughed and snuggled against him, caressing his cheek.

But he was serious. They made love again, and finally, regretfully, he said, "We need to get to the Marceau house."

She nodded. "And I need to get my book."

With a deep sigh, she rose and hurriedly gathered up her clothing and dressed as he did the same. She raced down the stairs before him, finding the book she wanted. She waited for him at the front door and then locked it behind them as they moved on to the main entrance.

Miss Lilly's door opened, and the woman peered out. "Take care, my young lovelies!" She looked at Ryder with a straight face. "I do hope your calls went well."

"My calls were great. Well, at least on my end, they went great."

He looked at Casey. She kicked him, hoping Miss Lilly couldn't see the motion.

As the door to Miss Lilly's apartment closed, Casey heard her laughing softly.

She sighed.

"Don't forget, we have her approval," Ryder reminded her.

They went out to the car.

"You know,"—he paused before opening her door—"premeditated is great, but it doesn't always have to be that way."

She didn't quite know how to respond as he ushered her into the car and closed the door. It took a few minutes of driving for her to form the question. "What does that mean?"

He looked at her and grinned. "You know where the door to my room is."

"Ryder, it's Stephanie's house—"

"I think she'd approve. But your call," he told her.

They'd reached the mansion.

"And now, Jackson Crow is here—"

"Jackson is always telling me to get a life." Ryder put the car into park and turned to her. "And what you said tonight is all too true. Life doesn't come with guarantees. For anyone."

"We should live," she said softly. "But I do need to read and shower. And you need to see Stephanie and Jackson—"

"And, therefore, we seize the moments," he said, grinning.

She might very well do that.

But then...

They approached the house. The historic home where Lena had lived.

And died.

Casey looked up at the house and made a silent vow.

She would be like Ryder. She'd never let it go. She'd do anything she could to help find whoever had stolen the beauty and life and goodness of Anthony and Lena Marceau—and William Marley.

Lena had come to her.

And she would not fail the gentle ghost.

Chapter 8

Ryder had poured his second cup of coffee in the morning when he turned to see that Lena's ghost was in the kitchen.

"Hello," he said softly.

"I'm learning, but I'm afraid I'm just slow as a ghost."

Stephanie walked in then with the baby. Annette immediately smiled and laughed and said, "Mama!"

Stephanie looked at Ryder with hope in her eyes. "She's here? Lena's here?" she asked.

"Tell her how much I love her, and thank you," Lena said, striding across the kitchen to take her sister in her arms.

"That's her, that's her! Right, this feeling?" Stephanie asked.

"It is," Ryder said softly.

Lena Marceau then wrapped her arms around her daughter. Annette giggled.

"Casey is here, right?" Lena asked Ryder anxiously.

He nodded. "She'll be down soon." He looked at Stephanie and said, "She asked about Casey."

Ryder had left her sleeping. They'd had a long night. He hadn't gotten much sleep himself, but he felt better this morning than he had in...a long time. Everything about this situation screamed that life—and love, human kindness, caring—were not to be taken for granted.

"Thank goodness," Lena said. "I never meant to make her life a nightmare. First, I popped in on her. And then, I popped out. Oh, Ryder. I am so sorry. It's just the strangest thing. I mean, I can feel it when I'm appearing and when I'm not, and it's almost like being alive. You have to rest sometimes to get your mojo going so the living can see you and...anyway."

"What's she saying?" Stephanie asked Ryder anxiously.

"She disappeared on us the other day, and she's explaining that it's difficult to appear when you're a new ghost," Ryder said. "I'm going to fill her in on what we're planning for the day." He turned back to where Lena stood. "I'm going with Stephanie to the board meeting today. She's going to insist they find another way to improve profits. There will be no charges above cost for necessary drugs. I'm going to watch for reactions from the foursome around her."

"But the baby—?" Lena said worriedly.

"That will be me," Jackson Crow said, entering the kitchen. "Lena, I'm Jackson Crow, field director for—"

"Oh, I know who you are," Lena said and smiled. "And you see me so clearly and hear me, and...well, of course, you do. Ryder told me all about you when he started with the Krewe. He was so excited. I didn't understand. In life, I had what Steph has, a sense, but nothing more. But I believed Ryder and I was so happy when he found work with people like him. But—wait! You're going to watch the baby?"

"I have two children of my own, thank you very much. I can play an excellent game of This Little Piggy Went to Market with a variety of ages. Annette and I will be fine," Jackson assured her.

"Plus, he has a Glock and is an excellent marksman. Not to mention, we'll still have one of the friends I hired to watch the cameras, and our suspects will be in the CBD," Ryder reminded Stephanie. "I'll be with you—every second," he told her.

Lena shook her head.

"What about Casey? I never meant to—I was just getting so desperate. But she's in danger now, too."

"We're going to see her to the shop. She'll be there with her friends and co-workers and Detective Braxton Wild."

"The detective believes in all this now?" Stephanie asked.

"He's known about ghosts for a while now. Comes with the territory of knowing about the Krewe. And he always did believe that what went on with Anthony and Lena was suspicious. He just didn't have anywhere else to go," Ryder said. "And the case is now in the hands of the FBI. So, you'll have us, and Braxton and the NOPD on this until it's solved."

Stephanie sank into a chair and looked around the table. "Thank you," she said. Then tears formed in her eyes, and she said softly, "Hug me again, Lena. Hug me, please. I miss you so much. So very, very much."

"Oh, Steph. I miss you too," Lena said and hugged her sister.

Jackson cleared his throat. "I'm here with Annette. The rest of you need to get going. Casey should be delivered safely to the French Quarter, and then Ryder and Stephanie need to get to the Marceau offices."

"I'll go up and make sure that Casey is ready," Lena said.

He hadn't wanted to move.

"I'm taking the baby to the safe room. If anything should happen, she'll be protected," Jackson murmured. He looked at Ryder, shaking his head. "This operation never took brawn. They play on people. Anthony was either pushed off the building after being lured to the roof or was told it was his life or Lena's or the baby's. I don't believe anyone will be getting through me."

"I don't believe so either," Ryder assured.

"But my baby is the key," Lena whispered. "She was always going to grow up privileged. Anthony and I wanted so badly to continue with Elijah's legacy, using all he had for good. I knew I could trust Stephanie to raise her. Anthony and I chose Stephanie and asked her the day the baby was born... We never thought we were putting her in the path of homicidal maniacs."

The killer—or killers—aren't maniacs, Ryder thought. They had a clear agenda. A takeover of Marceau Industries. They were organized, devious, and cunning.

"Lena, stay with us and have faith in us," Ryder said.

She smiled. "I do have faith in you," she said. "So..."

"We begin the day," Ryder said.

* * * *

Lena was back.

Casey saw the woman's ghost floating up the stairs just as she came down the hallway.

"Casey!" Lena said.

"Hey. You're good, huh?"

"Well, I'm dead, but I'm a stronger ghost now."

"I'm so sorry—"

"I'm joking. I mean, it's not a joke, just...well, a sense of humor helps us get through almost anything, huh?"

"True," Casey said softly. A sense of humor was...human.

Love, enjoyment, friends—all of those were human gifts. Longing to be held...

And to take it other places. That was human, too. *And okay*, she told herself.

The situation remained tense and dire. But it was okay to have had a beautiful night. She'd awoken feeling as if the sun were radiating through her and from her.

Lena's ghost hugged her, and she felt the strange yet comforting almost-there sensation. "I can't apologize to you enough—"

"Lena, it's all right. I've met wonderful, interesting people. And Detective Wild will be looking after me all day. Everything is good."

"'Sundrops, lollipops, and rainbows,'" Lena said dryly. Then she grinned. "Lemon drops! I always loved them. I still feel like I smell them now and then. Anyway, I'm holding us up. Time to go."

The baby was safely with Jackson.

Stephanie and Casey got into the car with Ryder, and Casey offered Stephanie the front passenger's seat.

"Lena is still here, isn't she?" Stephanie asked. When Ryder nodded, she added, "I'll sit with my sister." She crawled into the back and asked, "Lena can hear me, right?"

"She can," Ryder assured her.

"Lena, give me another hug. I love hugs," she said. Then, as Ryder pulled the car out into traffic, she said, "I can feel hugs. I can't do what you two can, but I can feel hugs."

Casey was happy as they drove to the French Quarter, where, while it was almost ten, there was still parking available.

Ryder wanted to make sure that Detective Wild was at the store.

He was. The detective greeted Ryder and Stephanie and had a special smile for Casey, telling her it was going to be a great day. He planned to sit in one of the chairs and look at the art and smile at all the people who came in. "I've been by here before. We'll get your friend to play and enjoy some good music," he said. But then he looked at Stephanie, his expression full of remorse. "I swear, we tried everything in our power."

Stephanie smiled at him. "I know. It's okay. I had nothing, either. Only the fact I knew my sister."

Lena's ghost gave Detective Wild a hug. He shivered.

"This is a really good guy," Lena said. "I know he tried to do the right thing."

"All right. If all is well, we're going to head over to the Central

Business District and the Marceau building," Ryder said, but he was looking at Casey.

Had she really only known him for two days? Had they really just spent an incredible night together?

A *premeditated* night?

She wanted to touch his face. She wanted to respond to the light—and the worry—in his eyes. She refrained.

He didn't. He pulled her into his arms and held her for a minute, then lifted her chin and tenderly kissed her lips.

"They'll know," Casey whispered.

"Yeah, they will," he answered.

They were both startled when Stephanie and Detective Wild—and Lena's ghost—applauded.

"I could have told you that you two would hit it off. In fact, I was going to bring you here, Ryder, the next time you came to see me. At least...well, I put Casey in danger, but at least I put the two of you together," Lena said happily.

"And now, we will get going," Ryder said.

"You need to open the door to the shop," Detective Wild said. "They frown on police opening doors without probable cause."

"Yes, yes, of course," Casey said. She turned the bolts as Ryder and Stephanie turned to go back to the car.

Ryder turned again and waved. Casey waved back. She wondered if she'd have a chance—with Detective Wild in the shop—to tell Lauren she'd taken her up on the concept of premeditated sex, and it had proven to be an excellent idea.

She walked in and told Detective Wild to make himself at home. He did. He looked around and enjoyed the art and the little souvenirs before sitting down in one of the chairs by the coffee service. Casey pulled up the computer and unlocked the cash register and card reader.

She noted it was after ten, and neither Lauren nor Jared had arrived.

They were seldom late, but maybe they'd met up at ten to head to a music venue. They did that now and then.

She was rearranging a jewelry display when her phone rang.

She didn't usually answer numbers she didn't know, but with Lauren and Jared both running late, she was worried.

"Hello?" she said.

"Miss Nicholson, don't hang up, and don't let that cop in there know anything is wrong at all. Just listen..."

The voice, coming through a distortion machine, broke off.

Then, she heard a scream. A terrible shriek of pain. And then Lauren's voice, "Casey, don't do whatever it is...they can't get away with it. They can't—"

"No."

The word came out as a whisper.

"Shut the hell up and quick! It would be so easy for me to kill her in the blink of an eye. You'd better not even make the kind of face that cop can read. I *will* kill her. I have a knife at her throat. If you tell the police? You may be fine. But I promise you, this little artist lady will be dead. Escape the cop somehow in the next few minutes. Get to the cemetery. And if you alert anyone—cops or FBI—we'll know. Do you want to hear the guy scream, too? I can make that happen. Get out of the shop and get to the cemetery unseen if you want these two to live."

Whoever it was hung up.

Casey stood there, frozen. She sank onto the stool behind the counter and tried to remain impassive.

This was how they got away with murder. They used a person's loved ones against them.

Casey had known that. And she knew that obeying the voice would be doing exactly what they wanted.

Be at the cemetery. New Orleans had dozens of them.

But she knew which one.

Call Ryder! her subconscious screamed.

She wanted to call him. Desperately. But someone was watching. And she knew she couldn't risk Lauren's life. Or Jared's.

She couldn't save her own...to risk theirs.

* * * *

"None of this has made any sense to me," Stephanie said. She was still riding in back. Ryder had assured her that he didn't mind looking like her chauffeur. "I mean, why would they want to get rid of all of us? Oh, I know those guys want to increase the prices on a lot of necessary drugs. But still, if something happens to Annette, it's not like the money goes to one person."

"Stephanie, do you remember if Anthony—or you, Lena—ever offended any of them personally?" Ryder asked as he drove. They'd been over the question before with Stephanie, but it didn't hurt to revisit the situation. Stephanie had been so lost and in such deep mourning when Lena died, she hadn't been thinking straight.

Lena might remember more now.

"Anthony was the nicest man in the world," Lena said. "He was so careful never to offend anyone."

"I can't think of anything," Stephanie said and then sighed. "I do know Barton Quincy thought Anthony was a flake. I heard him telling Anthony one time that he couldn't run a major corporation and act like St. Theresa at the same time."

"But Barton wouldn't just get everything," Lena protested. "Not even Justin would get everything, and he's a Marceau. And besides, Justin isn't like those guys. He's a free spirit."

Stephanie couldn't hear Lena, but her mind must have worked along the same lines. "Not Justin. I can't see it, I just can't."

"Money can do very strange things to people. And I don't think one person could have managed all this alone," Ryder said.

"Conspiracy theory?" Stephanie asked. "Seriously, Ryder. You think that many people can be that horrible?"

"If frightened for their own well-being, possibly," Ryder said.

"But all four of them?" Stephanie asked.

"Maybe not. I don't know. But I believe with my whole heart that at least one of them is guilty. None of this makes any sense at all otherwise," Ryder said. "Maybe one is seriously psychotic—death means nothing to them."

"Trust me, it means something," Lena said bitterly.

"When you have a person like that, and others who have an agenda and are willing to go along with something heinous if they don't have to perform any bloody acts themselves, you can easily have a conspiracy."

"Only one man threatened me and forced me to take the pills," Lena murmured.

"And we're back to the fact that the property video went blank at just the right time. And one of these guys must have figured out a way into the house. Maybe they managed to copy Anthony's keys and get code information off his phone... I don't know." Ryder grimaced.

At the Marceau offices in the CBD, they headed straight for the meeting room.

As they paused to check in with the receptionist, Lena murmured, "I'm going on ahead, to see what they're up to."

Stephanie chatted a minute with the receptionist while she checked to make sure the other board members had arrived and were going to the conference room. She was still talking when Lena's ghost came back to Ryder.

"This is going to be interesting. I heard Barton Quincy talking to Larry Swenson. He was saying that someone had 'gone off the rails.' That the 'idiot believes in ghosts!' Then they said they had suspected all along that 'she' needed to be taken care of, that 'she' shouldn't have been on it or that they should have dealt with 'her' earlier. Ryder, it doesn't sound like they're talking about Casey. So, who could they be talking about?"

He glanced at Lena and pulled his phone from his jacket pocket, pretending he'd gotten a phone call.

"There's only one other person I can think of...someone who could have helped them in what they needed to do for the right sum. Don't mock my conspiracy theories, cousin."

"Ryder, we can go on in now," Stephanie said.

They walked down a hallway toward the conference room.

Ryder was just about to enter when the phone he was still holding rang.

It was Braxton.

"Ryder, I swear I don't know how Casey did it, but..."

"Did what?"

"She's gone. Casey is gone. Her friends and co-workers never showed up for work. No one took her, Ryder. I know that much. She was here with me, and she stepped out to clean something off a window, and then...she was gone. No one took her. She ran. Away from me. On purpose."

Ryder felt his heart flip, and a burning sensation cascaded through him.

Fear.

He looked through the glass wall enclosure of the conference room, thinking that one of the four members besides Stephanie had to be absent.

But they were all there. Barton Quincy was at one end of the table. Justin was next to him, talking to him earnestly. Larry Swenson was sitting back, playing with his pen and looking bored. Harry Miller was writing notes on a pad.

If they were all there...

It still had to be someone connected.

She. The someone who was going off the rails.

He grabbed Stephanie by the shoulders. "Get in there. Be tough. Carry out the agenda just as we planned. I'm sending cops, and unless they get you out of the offices, you're going to be fine. Don't let them tell you the baby is in danger, or that I'm in danger or anything. Don't believe any threat if it comes to it, and don't leave the offices. You understand? Hang tough."

Workers were busy at desks in the main room, and the conference room was visible to all of them through the glass.

"Lena is with me?" Stephanie asked.

Ryder nodded.

"I won't leave her," Lena promised.

Ryder nodded again. He could hear Braxton, still on the line, calling his name. He put his phone back to his ear as he left the offices. "I need police at the Marceau offices, Braxton. Now. Those bastards can't try anything against Stephanie. I'm going after Casey."

"But where? I ran down the streets, Ryder, I swear. I didn't want to fail you. I called it in. She must have moved like lightning, and she knows how to zig and zag these streets and is aware of every little nook and cranny to hide in if a cop comes. I've got the city searching. I don't see how you're going to find her—"

"I will," Ryder said. "I will. Because I think I know where she's headed."

"I'll get the force out—"

"No. We can't. Not if everyone is going to come out of this alive. Just get here. Stephanie is in danger. I'll find Casey," he said.

He was already running out to his car.

He used his emergency vehicle lighting to make it through the French Quarter to Rampart.

Then he turned the lights off.

And prayed he was right.

Chapter 9

Casey ran, dodging tourists, glad they were closer to Esplanade than Canal. There seemed to be more tourists towards Canal and Jackson Square, but she was running away from there and the river toward Tremé. As she ran, she heard a jazz band playing, caught the sound of laughter and applause, and thought about the city—the unique architecture, the beauty of the cathedral, the colors, the laughter, and the unique décor that made up New Orleans. She felt the *life* of the city and kept running, arguing with herself all the while.

Whoever this is will just kill them all.

She was a psychology major. She would use psychology. If she didn't save her own life, it would be okay if they at least let Jared and Lauren go.

She ran almost all the way to Rampart and paused to catch her breath. The first order of business had been to escape Detective Braxton Wild. She was sorry for what she had done to him. He'd been there to protect her. He was nice, determined. He'd just never expected the woman he was supposed to be guarding to turn on him and run.

She took several deep breaths and started off again, this time at a quick walk. Could this person really have eyes everywhere? Would they have known if she had spoken to Detective Wild? But what if he'd tried to stop her? What if his interference had caused Lauren's death?

Again, and most logical, what if she got there and the murderer just killed all three of them?

That was definitely possible. But...

She had no choice. And she knew just how Lena had felt the day she had taken pills rather than watch her baby die.

There was still a ways to go. She crossed Rampart and quickly ran down a side street. She suddenly saw several police cars and wondered if they might be looking for her. Detective Wild would have likely called in her disappearance immediately.

But she bypassed them and reached the cemetery, running through the entrance as fast as she could. Like most cemeteries in the city, it had been laid out in lanes with small mausoleums lining each side, and occasional patches with in-ground burials, wall vaults or *ovens*, and single, aboveground tombs.

She knew the way to where she needed to be.

The gates were open. The Marley family mausoleum had not been properly resealed since William had been exhumed.

But she didn't head straight there *or* to the Marceau tomb. She was probably a fool. She remained torn, wondering how many killers were involved, if they really would have known if she had spoken to Detective Wild, and where they were now...

Did they know she was coming? That she was here?

She edged around the vault in front of her, trying to determine if she had been right about her destination. Did the killer want her here? And did the killer really hold Lauren and Jared?

Tangled vines surrounded the tomb, but she carefully crept around it. As she was doing so, she realized that she was being followed. Someone was behind her.

She reached into her bag, wishing she had a gun—and that she knew how to use one—and sought her phone.

She stopped and swung around, holding her cell high.

Someone stood in front of her, entirely clad in black like a child who had found a black bedsheet with which to play ghost.

Man? Woman? A smaller person, she thought. *Medium in stature but small for a man.*

"You're holding a cell phone on me?" the person demanded. The voice was amused and still coming to her distorted.

"I have the FBI on speed dial. You make a move toward me, my finger twitches, and they're all over you in two seconds."

How had this tiny person held Lauren and Jared and caused Lauren to scream?

Easy. He or she held a small gun in one hand.

And a large, glinting knife in the other.

"You let them go this instant. And you're an idiot. If you kill me, it won't get you any closer to Stephanie and the baby. It will only get you caught."

"You didn't talk to the cop. I know you didn't."

"They're closing in on you anyway."

"Oh, they'll never get to the bottom of it."

"I want to see Lauren and Jared."

"You'll see them. You just need to get into the tomb."

"No. I need to see them out here. I will hit speed dial. If we're all going to die, so are you."

If she kept this person talking, was she buying time? Detective Wild would have called Ryder by now. The police would be scouring the city.

But would anyone know to look in a small, almost-forgotten cemetery in Tremé?

"Why are you after me anyway?" she demanded. "I'm not a Marceau!"

"You know," the black-draped creature told her. "You know... Lena talked about you. She said you were amazing. I've—I've felt things. The bitch came back. Lena came back. And she came back to you. Eventually, you'll know, and you're going to tell them what happened and—"

"You think Lena came back? If I knew, I would have told them by now. Listen, no one knows who you are. Let my friends go. Let me go. I mean, I don't know how you pulled the rest of it off—"

"Me? Oh, not alone, my dear. We all played our parts. All for one and one for all. That's the only way you can ever trust anyone. Absolute loyalty comes when anyone is in danger of the death penalty. When the guilt is shared evenly. Ah, the challenges were great. The danger was great. But the rewards...endless. We all had alibis, absolutely ironclad. And there you have it."

Suddenly, it all made sense.

Keep her talking, keep her talking! she told herself.

"I see. Well, I'd watch it if I were you," Casey said.

"What are you talking about? You need to get in that tomb. That's where you'll find your friends."

"So you can shoot us all? That's not such a great idea either. A small cemetery...you figured no one comes here. No one will hear the shots. But that's a small enclosure. You're a small woman. If you want to kill me, you didn't come up with the best idea. I'm surprised the foursome let you in on this. I mean, whoever managed to get William Marley chock-full of cocaine to induce a heart attack...that was brilliant. Even if there had been an autopsy, how do you prove that someone forced him to overdose?

And killing Anthony? Lure him to the roof, and he falls over. No cameras, no one there, and it was probably staged to look like an accident or a suicide. If there had been a stray weather chopper or someone up on a taller building, it could have even appeared that Anthony was going to jump, and they were trying to talk him down."

"Foursome?"

"Well, they paid you, that foursome. Obviously. I guess your part in it all—for a handsome reward—was to see that one of them was able to get in, cut the video system, and go after Lena. That didn't take a rocket scientist. Threaten a baby, and a mother will do almost anything."

"You think you're so smart. It wasn't a foursome."

"Barton Quincy approached you, right?" Casey asked pleasantly.

"No, Miss Smarty Pants. Larry approached me. He said Anthony and Lena were ruining the company, and we'd all wind up on the streets if things were done their way. I worked my rear off for years for those people. Member of the family, they called me. Lena never even trusted me with Annette. She was always with that kid. Anthony barely knew I existed. Such good people! I was nothing to them. I was like the air. So, when Larry came to me and said he needed to get into the house and told me what he was going to pay me to help, I made sure he got in."

"Interesting that you felt that way. I saw how kind Stephanie was to you. But let's see. Barton Quincy warned you to make sure you were at your book club. Did you know then that he was going to kill Lena? Did you know about William Marley or Anthony?"

She shrugged. "I suspected, but... Stop it. And that family—not nice! They were patronizing. You need to get into the tomb."

"*You* need to figure out another plan. While you're shooting one of us, the other two will jump you. The tomb is too tight. So, two of us are dead, but so are you," Casey said.

"You think you're so smart!" Gail Reeves screamed and ripped off her mask and voice modulator. "You thought that up all by yourself. Sorry, it won't happen that way. Barton told me you're just a nut job despite how Lena said she loved your store and you. She said there was something so special about you. That you saw things."

"And you're trying to kill me—without permission from the guys—because you think Lena's ghost will tell me everything? Oh, Gail. Lena didn't even know you were the one who let her killer in. Who was it by the way? Justin?"

Gail waved her gun in the air. "Justin? Don't be an idiot. I don't think he could successfully set out to kill a cockroach. Justin wasn't in on this."

"Who killed Lena?"

"Who cares if you know? You know I will kill you. Larry took care of William. Harry Miller was responsible for seeing that Anthony went off the roof. And Barton Quincy took care of Lena—and he was anxious to do it."

"But they don't know what you're doing now, do they? Because if you weren't freaked out by the fact that I saw Lena's ghost—I do see her, by the way—you'd never have made this mistake. And it is a mistake. It will bring the cops down on all of you like locusts."

Gail Reeves smiled. She was nothing like a kindly grandmother.

There was malice—and lunacy—in her eyes.

"I have my money. I'll be long gone. Go, get into the tomb. If you die like a nice girl, I might let your friends live."

She will never let anyone live, Casey thought.

But she was trying to buy time. Heading for the tomb could buy her more.

"Lena, hey! There you are," she said.

Lena wasn't there, but Casey wanted to see the effect her words had on Gail Reeves.

Gail glared at her.

But as Casey reached the gate, it began swinging as if there were a breeze. She frowned.

Lena had gone to the board meeting. Could she be here? If she was, did that mean Ryder was here, too?

But it wasn't Lena. Casey saw the ghost of a World War II soldier by the gate. Given his uniform, he had been United States Air Force.

She blinked. A second ghost. One helping her.

This time, she wouldn't pass out. She was fighting for her life.

"Dante Marceau, Miss Nicholson. Friend of Lena. I'm sorry to say I didn't make it back from Normandy, but I'm delighted to be here today to help you in any way I can. Lena has told me all about you."

Yes, of course, Lena had friends now who were ghosts.

"Thank you!" Casey said aloud.

It was almost pitch-black inside the tomb. Only a small stained-glass window at the rear allowed in shards of colored light.

It was enough.

Gail Reeves had managed to get Jared and Lauren inside. They were tied back to back and seated just below the stained-glass window.

Gail had used her blade on Lauren, leaving a bloody slash across her cheek.

Her friends both looked at Casey as if they were heartsick. Terrified, but sick that she had come.

That she would ultimately join their fate. Casey closed her eyes briefly. Her life didn't flash before her. She smelled the moldy scent of the tomb, saw the niche where William Marley's body had recently lain. The floor was dusty, spiderwebs teased the walls and crypts. It was truly the home of the dead.

"Go, go, get in!" Gail said harshly.

"Wait!" Casey said. "She's here. Lena is here. Be careful—"

The gate didn't just jiggle or sway. It slammed hard, separating Casey from Gail. Unnerved, Gail fired a shot. It slammed into stone.

She took better aim to fire again.

But the gun was suddenly ripped cleanly from her hand as Ryder leapt out from behind a neighboring tomb, his movements smooth and easy.

Gail screamed as her fingers twisted, and she fell to the ground in front of the mausoleum. But she bolted up, the knife in her hand, raving mad as she lunged at Ryder. He caught her wrist and grabbed the knife. When she tried to strike him, he ducked and struck back.

"Ryder, thank God!" Casey breathed, starting to come out of the tomb.

"No, no, get back in there for a minute. Let me get Gail in there and then close the gate," Ryder said.

"What—?"

"They know I left. And they know Gail is a whack job."

Casey edged back into the tomb, hunkering down as Ryder lifted Gail's unconscious body, slid her in, and closed the gate. Then, he disappeared.

Casey moved closer to Lauren and Jared, bringing a finger to her lips in the strange and eerily colored darkness that was the realm of the dead.

"She's got to be here. I told you we needed to do something about her!"

Larry Swenson was doing the speaking.

"We needed her. We had to get to Stephanie and the baby, and she was our shot. If we can't kill them, this has all been for nothing."

Harry Miller was with Larry Swenson. They were walking through the graveyard, hurriedly coming toward the tomb.

"What if the cops get here?" Larry asked.

"We lay it on Gail. Say we were getting suspicious. Barton should have been here, too, but he's always keeping himself out of the way. Bastard! Thinks if we get ourselves killed, he'll take the whole prize. Then, he'd have to kill Justin Marceau, too. And he hates getting his hands dirty," Harry said disgustedly.

"He got his hands dirty. He killed Lena," Larry mumbled.

"He thought he could control her. When he couldn't...he really hated her."

The two were almost at the mausoleum.

Ryder suddenly stepped out in front of them.

"Gentlemen," he said. "I'm afraid you're going to have to stop there. You're under arrest for murder."

Casey inched forward, moving over the prone shape of Gail Reeves.

She saw both men draw guns.

But Ryder, who had sounded so easygoing, who hadn't even been holding his Glock, got both men before they could fire their weapons. Larry Swenson spun around and fell as a bullet ripped through his shoulder, and Harry Miller screamed like a crazed banshee as his hand was shattered.

By then, cops and FBI agents were running through the cemetery. Ryder opened the door to the tomb, and Casey leapt up, anxious to free her tied and gagged friends. Casey hugged Lauren and Jared as the pair cried with relief. They garbled out words to explain how Gail had been hiding in the back of Lauren's car and had forced them here at gunpoint, and then bound and forced them to gag each other.

Gail had secured them together in the tomb and then cut Lauren so she would scream, and Casey would come.

It was bedlam.

Lauren and Jared were taken away in an ambulance to be checked out, and so Lauren could receive stitches.

Larry Swenson, Harry Miller, and Gail Reeves were taken away.

Ghosts milled about and watched the activity. Lena Marceau stood with Dante Marceau, the apparitions arm-in-arm.

"I don't think this place has ever seen so much life," she said, grinning.

Braxton Wild walked over to Casey and hugged her tightly. "You're all right. You're all right!" Then he frowned. "Young lady, don't you ever do such a thing again."

"I'm sorry, Detective Wild," she said.

He grinned. "Call me Braxton. I hear we're going to Frenchman Street together later tonight to listen to some kickass bands."

Casey smiled at him. "Okay by me."

Braxton looked at Ryder and said, "The police picked up Barton Quincy. He's busy blaming it all on the housekeeper, claiming innocence. And we also have Justin, who is also claiming innocence."

"From everything I heard, Justin *is* innocent," Casey told him.

"Well, we'll see about talking to him and letting him go this afternoon. The others...they'll face state and federal charges." He looked at Ryder. "You could have killed them. You let them off easy."

Ryder shook his head. "They'll be in a maximum-security prison. They'll never get out. They need to suffer a long, long time for what they did."

Ryder put an arm around Casey. "Should we be going out tonight? Are you all right? What about Lauren and Jared?"

"Yes, we should go out tonight." She grimaced. "Life is short. Let's live it," she said softly.

Epilogue

They didn't go out that night. There was far too much paperwork. And too many people who had to understand a great deal. Jackson worried at first that they might have trouble in court, but they quickly learned that every one of the conspirators was ready to turn on the other.

They all wanted deals.

The best the conspirators would get was the death sentence taken off the table.

No, they didn't go out that night. Or the next. But now, a few weeks later, it was finally time to put everything behind them and celebrate.

Even Stephanie came. It was going to be a long time before she trusted leaving Annette with anyone, but there *was* one babysitter she had come to trust and love.

Jackson Crow.

And Jackson had insisted that Stephanie get out.

Justin Marceau was with them. He and Stephanie were going to have a hell of a time trying to remake the company and find good people to help them. But they both believed that good people were out there. And Justin was both terrified and grateful.

He knew he would have eventually been on the hit list.

"Really, the only way it broke was Gail Reeves going crazy believing in ghosts," Justin said. He shook his head, and Casey smiled. "Some people."

Jared and Lauren came. And Braxton had ridden with Ryder and Casey. Jared even sat in with a few of the bands they stopped to see, and it was great to see him happy and in his element.

Toward the end of the evening, and after much thought and

discussion with Ryder, Casey asked Lauren and Jared what they thought about taking over the shop. It was their shop, really. They were the art and the music.

"But," Lauren told her, "you were always the beautiful mind."

"I knew it from the moment I walked into the shop," Lena's ghost said, and Casey smiled, though the others couldn't hear Lena. "You were, but these two are its heart. Just like Ryder is yours, and you are his." Casey smiled wider.

"So you're moving in with Ryder?" Jared asked.

She nodded. "But we both love NOLA. We'll be back."

The night with friends was wonderful. The next day was better.

They went back to the cemetery—Jackson, Stephanie, Annette, Ryder, and Casey.

They stood by the tomb as other ghosts made appearances.

Lena had shared with Casey that she'd sensed Anthony's presence when the arrests were made in the cemetery, but nothing since. Still, she had a feeling she might go with him when the time was right.

It was daytime, but it seemed a streak of light stronger than the sun shone down by the tomb. And a misty, almost golden image of a man appeared in that ray of light.

He reached out a hand to Lena.

Lena paused, and a collective gasp of fear went through the group as the ghostly mother managed to take hold of her child and then race to the light with the baby.

"Annette," Stephanie whispered.

But the group seemed to be just a burst of light for a minute as Lena and Anthony held their beloved daughter.

Then, Lena ran back with the baby, hugging Stephanie and returning the child to her guardian's arms.

"I love you. Please understand. Please love her as I would. As I will always love you both. And everyone, thank you. Thank you!" she said.

The light was gone, and Lena with it. Stephanie sobbed softly, and Ryder set his arm around her. He assured her that he and Casey would stick around for a while. There would be more paperwork and additional things about the case to untangle. And Casey knew he would do whatever was necessary to make sure everything was locked up tight, that the board members and Gail got what was coming to them, and that his family was never harmed again.

Later that night, lying together, Ryder seemed thoughtful.

"Are you sure you don't mind picking up and leaving, giving up everything to come with me?" he asked her, not for the first time.

She smiled and stroked his face.

"Jared and Lauren will be fine with the store. Jennie Sanders will know she has special powers now." She laughed. "Someone tall, dark, and dangerously handsome *did* enter my life to sweep me off my feet. We have learned so much about death...and life. Let's seize it and live it," she said.

He smiled, straddling her.

"You do have a beautiful mind. And...hmm. A beautiful rest of you, too."

She laughed softly. "Thank you. And as for life..."

"Let's get to it!"

He kissed her.

Life.

She had come close to losing it. She had discovered that she could help someone who had lost it. And now...

It was a gift. And she would cherish every minute of it.

Especially with Ryder.

* * * *

Also from 1001 Dark Nights and Heather Graham, discover Blood Night, Haunted Be the Holidays, Hallow Be The Haunt, Crimson Twilight, When Irish Eyes Are Haunting, All Hallows Eve, and Blood on the Bayou.

Sign up for the 1001 Dark Nights Newsletter
and be entered to win a Tiffany Key necklace.

There's a contest every month!

Go to www.1001DarkNights.com to subscribe.

**As a bonus, all subscribers can download
FIVE FREE exclusive books!**

Discover 1001 Dark Nights Collection Seven

THE BISHOP by Skye Warren
A Tanglewood Novella

TAKEN WITH YOU by Carrie Ann Ryan
A Fractured Connections Novella

DRAGON LOST by Donna Grant
A Dark Kings Novella

SEXY LOVE by Carly Phillips
A Sexy Series Novella

PROVOKE by Rachel Van Dyken
A Seaside Pictures Novella

RAFE by Sawyer Bennett
An Arizona Vengeance Novella

THE NAUGHTY PRINCESS by Claire Contreras
A Sexy Royals Novella

THE GRAVEYARD SHIFT by Darynda Jones
A Charley Davidson Novella

CHARMED by Lexi Blake
A Masters and Mercenaries Novella

SACRIFICE OF DARKNESS by Alexandra Ivy
A Guardians of Eternity Novella

THE QUEEN by Jen Armentrout
A Wicked Novella

BEGIN AGAIN by Jennifer Probst
A Stay Novella

VIXEN by Rebecca Zanetti
A Dark Protectors/Rebels Novella

SLASH by Laurelin Paige
A Slay Series Novella

THE DEAD HEAT OF SUMMER by Heather Graham
A Krewe of Hunters Novella

WILD FIRE by Kristen Ashley
A Chaos Novella

MORE THAN PROTECT YOU by Shayla Black
A More Than Words Novella

LOVE SONG by Kylie Scott
A Stage Dive Novella

CHERISH ME by J. Kenner
A Stark Ever After Novella

SHINE WITH ME by Kristen Proby
A With Me in Seattle Novella

And new from Blue Box Press:

TEASE ME by J. Kenner
A Stark International Novel

FROM BLOOD AND ASH by Jennifer L. Armentrout
A Blood and Ash Novel

QUEEN MOVE by Kennedy Ryan

THE HOUSE OF LONG AGO by Steve Berry and MJ Rose
A Cassiopeia Vitt Adventure

THE BUTTERFLY ROOM by Lucinda Riley

A KINGDOM OF FLESH AND FIRE by Jennifer L. Armentrout
A Blood and Ash Novel

Discover More Heather Graham

Blood Night: A Krewe of Hunters Novella

Any member of the Krewe of Hunters is accustomed to the strange. And to conversing now and then with the dead.

For Andre Rousseau and Cheyenne Donegal, an encounter with the deceased in a cemetery is certainly nothing new.

But this year, Halloween is taking them across the pond—unofficially.

Their experiences in life haven't prepared them for what's to come.

Cheyenne's distant cousin and dear friend Emily Donegal has called from London. Murder has come to her neighborhood, with bodies just outside Highgate Cemetery, drained of blood.

The last victim was found at Emily's doorstep, and evidence seems to be arising not just against her fiancé, Eric, but against Emily, too. But Emily isn't just afraid of the law—many in the great city are beginning to believe that the historic Vampire of Highgate is making himself known, aided and abetted by adherents. Some are even angry and frightened enough to believe they should take matters into their own hands.

Andre and Cheyenne know they're in for serious trouble when they arrive, and they soon come to realize that the trouble might be deadly not just for Emily and Eric, but for themselves as well.

There's help to be found in the beautiful and historic old cemetery.

And as All Hallows Eve looms, they'll be in a race against time, seeking the truth before the infamous vampire has a chance to strike again.

* * * *

Haunted Be the Holidays: A Krewe of Hunters Novella

When you're looking for the victim of a mysterious murder in a theater, there is nothing like calling on a dead diva for help! Krewe members must find the victim if they're to discover the identity of a murderer at large, one more than willing to kill the performers when he doesn't like the show.

It's Halloween at the Global Tower Theatre, a fantastic and historic theater owned by Adam Harrison and run by spouses of Krewe members.

During a special performance, a strange actor makes an appearance in the middle of the show, warning of dire events if his murder is not solved before another holiday rolls around.

Dakota McCoy and Brodie McFadden dive into the mystery. Both have a. special talent for dealing with ghosts, but this one is proving elusive. With the help of Brodie's diva mother and his ever-patient father—who were killed together when a stage chandelier fell upon them—Dakota and Brodie set out to solve the case.

If they can't solve the murder quickly, there will be no Thanksgiving for the Krewe...

* * * *

Hallow Be the Haunt: A Krewe of Hunters Novella

Years ago, Jake Mallory fell in love all over again with Ashley Donegal—while he and the Krewe were investigating a murder that replicated a horrible Civil War death at her family's Donegal Plantation.

Now, Ashley and Jake are back—planning for their wedding, which will take place the following month at Donegal Plantation, her beautiful old antebellum home.

But Halloween is approaching and Ashley is haunted by a ghost warning her of deaths about to come in the city of New Orleans, deaths caused by the same murderer who stole the life of the beautiful ghost haunting her dreams night after night.

At first, Jake is afraid that returning home has simply awakened some of the fear of the past...

But as Ashley's nightmares continue, a body count begins to accrue in the city...

And it's suddenly a race to stop a killer before Hallow's Eve comes to a crashing end, with dozens more lives at stake, not to mention heart, soul, and life for Jake and Ashley themselves.

* * * *

Crimson Twilight: A Krewe of Hunters Novella

It's a happy time for Sloan Trent and Jane Everett. What could be happier than the event of their wedding? Their Krewe friends will all be there and the event will take place in a medieval castle transported brick by brick to the New England coast. Everyone is festive and thrilled... until the priest turns up dead just hours before the nuptials. Jane and Sloan must find the truth behind the man and the murder--the secrets of the living and the dead--before they find themselves bound for eternity--not in wedded bliss but in the darkness of an historical wrong and their own brutal deaths.

* * * *

When Irish Eyes Are Haunting: A Krewe of Hunters Novella

Devin Lyle and Craig Rockwell are back, this time to a haunted castle in Ireland where a banshee may have gone wild—or maybe there's a much more rational explanation—one that involves a disgruntled heir, murder, and mayhem, all with that sexy light touch Heather Graham has turned into her trademark style.

* * * *

All Hallows Eve: A Krewe of Hunters Novella

Salem was a place near and dear to Jenny Duffy and Samuel Hall -- it was where they'd met on a strange and sinister case. They never dreamed that they'd be called back. That history could repeat itself in a most macabre and terrifying fashion. But, then again, it was Salem at Halloween. Seasoned Krewe members, they still find themselves facing the unspeakable horrors in a desperate race to save each other-and perhaps even their very souls.

* * * *

Blood on the Bayou: A Cafferty & Quinn Novella

It's winter and a chill has settled over the area near New Orleans, finding a stream of blood, a tourist follows it to a dead man, face down in the bayou.

The man has been done in by a vicious beating, so violent that his skull has been crushed in.

It's barely a day before a second victim is found... once again so badly thrashed that the water runs red. The city becomes riddled with fear.

An old family friend comes to Danni Cafferty, telling her that he's terrified, he's certain that he's received a message from the Blood Bayou killer--It's your turn to pay, blood on the bayou.

Cafferty and Quinn quickly become involved, and--as they all begin to realize that a gruesome local history is being repeated--they find themselves in a fight to save not just a friend, but, perhaps, their very own lives.

About Heather Graham

New York Times and *USA Today* bestselling author, Heather Graham, majored in theater arts at the University of South Florida. After a stint of several years in dinner theater, back-up vocals, and bartending, she stayed home after the birth of her third child and began to write. Her first book was with Dell, and since then, she has written over two hundred novels and novellas including category, suspense, historical romance, vampire fiction, time travel, occult and Christmas family fare.

She is pleased to have been published in approximately twenty-five languages. She has written over 200 novels and has 60 million books in print. She has been honored with awards from booksellers and writers' organizations for excellence in her work, and she is also proud to be a recipient of the Silver Bullet Award from the International Thriller Writers and was also awarded the prestigious Thriller Master in 2016. She is also a recipient of the Lifetime Achievement Award from RWA. Heather has had books selected for the Doubleday Book Club and the Literary Guild, and has been quoted, interviewed, or featured in such publications as The Nation, Redbook, Mystery Book Club, People and USA Today and appeared on many newscasts including Today, Entertainment Tonight and local television.

Heather loves travel and anything that has to do with the water and is a certified scuba diver. She also loves ballroom dancing. Each year she hosts a ball or dinner theater raising money for the Pediatric Aids Society and in 2006 she hosted the first Writers for New Orleans Workshop to benefit the stricken Gulf Region. She is also the founder of "The Slush Pile Players," presenting something that's "almost like entertainment" for various conferences and benefits. Married since high school graduation and the mother of five, her greatest love in life remains her family, but she also believes her career has been an incredible gift, and she is grateful every day to be doing something that she loves so very much for a living.

Discover 1001 Dark Nights

HALLOW BE THE HAUNT by Heather Graham
DIRTY FILTHY FIX by Laurelin Paige
THE BED MATE by Kendall Ryan
NIGHT GAMES by CD Reiss
NO RESERVATIONS by Kristen Proby
DAWN OF SURRENDER by Liliana Hart

COLLECTION FIVE
BLAZE ERUPTING by Rebecca Zanetti
ROUGH RIDE by Kristen Ashley
HAWKYN by Larissa Ione
RIDE DIRTY by Laura Kaye
ROME'S CHANCE by Joanna Wylde
THE MARRIAGE ARRANGEMENT by Jennifer Probst
SURRENDER by Elisabeth Naughton
INKED NIGHTS by Carrie Ann Ryan
ENVY by Rachel Van Dyken
PROTECTED by Lexi Blake
THE PRINCE by Jennifer L. Armentrout
PLEASE ME by J. Kenner
WOUND TIGHT by Lorelei James
STRONG by Kylie Scott
DRAGON NIGHT by Donna Grant
TEMPTING BROOKE by Kristen Proby
HAUNTED BE THE HOLIDAYS by Heather Graham
CONTROL by K. Bromberg
HUNKY HEARTBREAKER by Kendall Ryan
THE DARKEST CAPTIVE by Gena Showalter

COLLECTION SIX
DRAGON CLAIMED by Donna Grant
ASHES TO INK by Carrie Ann Ryan
ENSNARED by Elisabeth Naughton
EVERMORE by Corinne Michaels
VENGEANCE by Rebecca Zanetti
ELI'S TRIUMPH by Joanna Wylde
CIPHER by Larissa Ione
RESCUING MACIE by Susan Stoker
ENCHANTED by Lexi Blake

TAKE THE BRIDE by Carly Phillips
INDULGE ME by J. Kenner
THE KING by Jennifer L. Armentrout
QUIET MAN by Kristen Ashley
ABANDON by Rachel Van Dyken
THE OPEN DOOR by Laurelin Paige
CLOSER by Kylie Scott
SOMETHING JUST LIKE THIS by Jennifer Probst
BLOOD NIGHT by Heather Graham
TWIST OF FATE by Jill Shalvis
MORE THAN PLEASURE YOU by Shayla Black
WONDER WITH ME by Kristen Proby
THE DARKEST ASSASSIN by Gena Showalter

Discover Blue Box Press

TAME ME by J. Kenner
TEMPT ME by J. Kenner
DAMIEN by J. Kenner
TEASE ME by J. Kenner
REAPER by Larissa Ione
THE SURRENDER GATE by Christopher Rice
SERVICING THE TARGET by Cherise Sinclair
THE LAKE OF LEARNING by Steve Berry and MJ Rose
THE MUSEUM OF MYSTERIES by Steve Berry and MJ Rose

On Behalf of 1001 Dark Nights,

Liz Berry, M.J. Rose, and Jillian Stein would like to thank ~

Steve Berry
Doug Scofield
Benjamin Stein
Kim Guidroz
Social Butterfly PR
Asha Hossain
Chris Graham
Chelle Olson
Kasi Alexander
Jessica Johns
Dylan Stockton
Richard Blake
and Simon Lipskar

Made in the USA
Middletown, DE
08 September 2020